IN THE LOVE OF TEXAS

A TOOMBS SULLIVAN ADVENTURE

BOOK FIVE

TOM PILGRIM

For information contact: info@outlawspublishing.com
Cover Art by Michael Thomas
Cover design by Outlaws Publishing LLC
Published by Outlaws Publishing LLC
July 2024
10987654321

Dedicated To My Father

Reverend William Arthur Pilgrim Who Took Me To See Many Cowboy Movies

Chapter 1

Toombs Sullivan ducked down between two horses. They were tied at the rail just to the left of the front door of the Fort Worth Bank.

He had heard a gun-shot coming from the bank. As he started toward the bank, he saw a woman running out of the door. She was screaming, as she ran right toward him.

"What is it?" he asked her.

"Two men! . . . . Robbing the bank! . . . . Bad men!"

Sullivan waited as his pulse quickened, his breathing became more rapid. They were coming out soon. He knew that. But what they did not know was that he was waiting on them.

He rehearsed in his mind what might unfold. There were two ways to do this. There was the easy way, and then there was the other easy way. They could come go with him peacefully, or go to the undertaker peacefully, and be at peace from now on. He did not really care which way they chose. It would be their choice. He would just as soon kill them right there for he had long since had enough of robbers, killers, bad men, Comanche Indians, Comancheros, and any other combination of any of that you might be able to think up.

Sullivan saw the door swing open as both men backed out of it with their backs to him. This was a good time for introductions.

"Just hold it right there! Put yore guns down slowly, and drop that bag quickly!"

Sullivan could tell the man on the right was saying something to the man on the left.

They turned with the intent of shooting him. Bad mistake.

Two shots rang out down the street. Two bad men hit the boardwalk, and rolled into the street.

The bank president, John Jacob Judson, peeped out of the door. When he saw the bad men lying in the street, he came on out. He looked at them, and then he looked at Sullivan. His eyes were wide open, and his mouth was as well.

Sullivan called out to him, "Anybody shot in there? Anybody hurt?"

"No," Judson managed to say. "They just shot a hole in my ceiling."

"Good," Sullivan said.

"No. It's not good. I got a hole in my ceiling now."

"Figures. Just be glad there's not one in you."

John Jacob Judson was speechless.

"Better pick up yore money before somebody else does, Mister Judson."

"Yes, of course, Mister Sullivan. Thanks. Thanks a lot for your good work today."

"It was easy."

Chapter 2

Toombs Sullivan sat in the sheriff's office in Fort Worth. One reason was he had nothing better to do. Another reason was because of the aggressive heat. Outside of town, people could see heat waves rising from the plains. Inside of town, the heat beat down on the city streets, causing old men to need to wipe the sweat from their brows at regular intervals, and old women to almost swoon.

Toombs Sullivan had decided it was time to ask Josephine Wells to marry him. They had talked about it many times, knew they would eventually, but never had done it. They had not only talked about it, they had thought about it, dreamed about it, dreamed of it, planned for it, anticipated it, but they just had never quite made that final decision. He had his work as a Texas Ranger that took him far and wide, being gone for weeks at a time. She had her work at her ranch, which could be all-consuming. But now the time had come. It was the year 1870.

It was time for Sullivan to settle down. He had spent four years traveling over a good part of Texas, from San Antonio southward during his first year as a Ranger, and then from Dallas north, east, and west. He had fought Comanches, which was the main purpose of the Rangers, protecting the people of the state from them and other Indians. He had also fought Comancheros, bank robbers, stage coach robbers, and killers. He had had enough of all that.

Though still young, these adventures all over Texas had taken their toll. It was the normal wear and tear for a Ranger. Those who lived long enough learned what chasing Indians can do to the body.

So now the time had come. Toombs Sullivan was a sworn-in Sheriff's Deputy in the city of Fort Worth, Texas.

Even though he knew leaving the Rangers was the thing to do, still it had been a difficult decision, and an even more difficult break to actually make. He was worried about how Captain Jack Rice would take it.

Jack Rice was in his mid-forties, maybe even a little older. Sullivan did not know. Asking Rice about his age was not the thing to do. But he had devoted his life to being a Ranger, with no thought or plan to ever take a wife. Would he understand what Sullivan was saying and why? He did not know. There was only one way to find out.

One morning, Sullivan walked into the office, and sat down in the chair right across from Captain Rice. He looked at him for a moment. Rice looked back, appearing to be ready to respond to whatever Sullivan was going to say.

Sullivan finally spoke, though the words did not come easy.

"Uh, Captain . . . . I need to talk to you about somethin'."

"I figured you did, being here and all."

"I have made a decision."

"I make'em all the time."

"I am going to marry Josephine."

"Oh, wonderful. Congratulations, and all that."

"Thanks, but it's the all that that is a problem."

"What's the problem?"

"I can't marry her, and be a Ranger at the same time. The two things don't go together. That's the why of me never doin' it sooner."

"What are you saying? Spit it out."

"I'm leaving the Rangers, Captain. I got to. No two ways to slice that."

"You sure now?"

"Yep. Been puttin' it off for a long time. Captain, I love Texas. I love bein' a Ranger. It's the best thing that has ever happened to me, far as what I could do and become, like that. But I also love Josephine. She needs me, and I need her, and I can't be a Ranger and a good husband both at the same time, ya know."

"I understand, Sullivan. I do. I once loved a girl. I was just startin' out as a Ranger. I wanted to marry her. But I saw what that would do to her. I could not do both,

I knew it. I gave her up. She said she understood. I don't know if she did or not. Met up with her one time years later. She married a lawyer. She had five kids, five boys, stair step like. Not marrying her was the best thing I could ever do for her, because I was not going to quit being a Ranger. Yeah, I understand. I hate to lose you now. No doubt about that. You been my right-hand man. You have served the state of Texas in the best possible way. But you go with my blessings. You do."

"Well, I appreciate all you have done for me. And I appreciate the Rangers taking me in when I first came to Texas. I was at a really low point, ya know. My wife and son died during the war, ya remember. I found their graves, and came out here out of desperation. I had no idea why. I just knew I was running away from it. Running from one love that was lost, I found another love. Texas."

"And now, another love. You are a lucky man indeed."

"Yes, Sir. I am."

"What will you do?"

"I found out the sheriff in Fort Worth needed a new Deputy. When I went over to see Josephine the other day, I stopped in, and he gave me the job. Me being a Ranger sealed the deal."

"What does she think about that?"

"I haven't told her yet. I'm going on over to see her right away."

"Good. If ya need us, we'll be around."

"So will I. Works both ways, ya know."

Chapter 3

When Sullivan arrived at Josephine's ranch, she heard him ride up, and went out to meet him. They embraced and kissed.

"What brings you over this way?"

"I need to talk to you. In a serious way."

"Let's sit on the porch out of the sun."

When they reached the porch, and were seated, Sullivan looked at Josephine. He took a moment to catch his breath.

"Josephine, it's time we got married. I love you, ya know that. We put it off too long. Now the time has come."

"What about your job? You have always said you did not want me married to a man the Indians might get instead of me."

"I'm leaving the Rangers. I love you more than the work."

"But you have always said you could never be a rancher."

"I got a job as a Deputy Sheriff in Fort Worth. It ain't but fifteen miles away. Some nights I'll have to stay there. Most nights I can come home. Here."

"If you're asking, the answer is yes, of course."

They both stood up at the same time, and hugged each other.

"Maybe I have a better idea," Josephine said. "What if I sell this ranch, and we both live in town."

"That's a big decision for you to make."

"No bigger than the one you made. It's called meeting in the middle."

"You're sure?"

"Sure, I'm sure. I was not ever cut out to chase a bunch of cows. I have been doing this because I fell into it, and really had no other choice. It's time to make a change for me as well. With what I'll get from this ranch, we'll be able to buy a house in town, and have lots of money left over. Besides, don't forget, my husband left me a good bit of money."

"So, you don't mind me being a town lawman?"

"A lawman is what you are. A cowman is what I am not. Not a cowfemale, cowwoman, neither. You can do what you love without all that travel all over God's creation."

"Some of the places where I been, I don't think God would even claim."

"I'm glad all of that is over. I died each time you went out. I only came back alive when I knew you were safely back."

"It's over, Josephine. It's all over. But that don't mean I will always be safe. There's killin' in towns. Bank robbers, natural born killers, drunk cowboys, they all are a danger, especially to a lawman. In town. It's just that there's not much travel. Except out in the county."

"I know. I understand all that. But I'll be with you this time. That's the difference."

"All right. I need to go back to Dallas, and close things out there. The sheriff is expecting me to start next week. I told him I would."

"Now, what's that sheriff's name?"

"Clay Morrison."

"Oh, yes."

"I'll see ya real soon. I'll contact the preacher in town about doing the wedding."

"Good. I'll send one of the boys to town to get a notice in the paper about this place being for sale, and also to deliver a letter to the bank about all the arrangements."

"I love you. Be careful," he said, as he kissed her goodbye.

"You be careful, Deputy."

When Sullivan arrived back in Dallas, he said goodbye to all of his Ranger friends, said goodbye to Captain Rice, turned in his Texas Ranger badge, got his final pay, paid a few bills around town, took his money out of the bank, gathered his personal items, and the next day he left Dallas, perhaps for good.

He rode west headed for a new life, or maybe it was a new chapter in his old life. Whatever it was, he knew he had made a break from one thing, and entered something else.

Josephine already had her eye on a house in Fort Worth. She had seen it a couple of times. It was a grand house on a little hill just north of the main street. It was large, two stories, painted white with four white columns out front, just like the old houses she loved back home in New Orleans. It was for sale, had been for almost a year, but no one in Fort Worth had either the money or the interest or the desire or whatever it is that makes a person want a particular house. Josephine had the money and the interest and the desire. She wanted that particular house. It had been owned by a man who was in the cotton business. He died of what must have been a stroke. His wife went back east. There were no children, no one who would inherit it. Josephine wanted it. She bought it.

That same week at another house, the parsonage where the Methodist parson, Reverend Elias Montgomery lived, Josephine Wells and Toombs Sullivan were married. It was a small wedding. The only ones attending were the parson and his wife, Ellabell. The parson performed the ceremony for free. Ellabell made a cake.

After the ceremony, the four of them stood around talking. They ate most of the cake.

13

Chapter 4

It was on that very hot day that Toombs Sullivan was sitting there in the sheriff's office, because he had nothing else to do, that he heard that one shot coming from down the street. He did not know where it came from.

He rushed out, and saw that lady who was doing all the screaming. That was when he ducked down between the two horses, and then shot the bank robbers. He shot both of them dead on the spot. They laid right there in the street, and never moved a muscle, not even a twitch, not one last breath.

Sullivan asked the gathering crowd if anybody knew who they were.

"Yeah, I do," said one of the older men who had to wipe the sweat off his brow at regular intervals. "That one rat thar is Colby Collins. Why, he growed up here abouts. Can't figure why he'd come in here, and rob this bank. That othern is a boy out of Alabama, name of Bobby Overdorf. He got a bad reputation here real quick, always making trouble. Bet he talked that Collins boy into doing this. It's a pity. Both so young."

"And both so dead," said an older lady who had been about to swoon because of the heat, but the momentary excitement had revived her.

"Well," said Sullivan, "somebody go get the undertaker."

"Here he comes," said that older man. "He don't miss a trick. He'll take'em under all right. Where he'll take'em, they ain't never comin' back."

Sullivan went back to the office to write down the particulars of the encounter. The sheriff was very strict about keeping good records of everything that happened. When he was finished writing their names in the book, along with the date and the cause of death, he decided to go home. It was late in the day by then, and it was almost supper time.

Sullivan walked over to the street that went up to the little hill where the big white house and Josephine awaited him. There were times when he could not believe he had married such a fine woman, and they lived together in such a fine house. But he knew it was true because he went home every night, and she was always there.

Sullivan entered the house, and walked straight back to the kitchen. It was a large room with a large cooking stove, and a fire place as well. The other side of the fireplace was in the large living room. If you wanted to, you might walk from one room into the other through the double fireplace. But neither of them ever wanted to. They would have had to stoop down too low.

"What's for supper?" he asked.

"Is that the first thing you are going to say to me?"

"Why, no. I love you very much. I missed you terribly all day. What's for supper?"

"Your favorites. Beef steak, potatoes, beans, bread, coffee."

"My favorites."

"Guess what?"

"What?"

"We have a buyer for the ranch."

"Wonderful. Who?"

"A nice couple. They have a small ranch near Marshall, but they want something bigger. They have two boys. And they are from Georgia, I understand."

"Well, this is good. I know you are relieved. I guess you are, right?"

"I am relieved. And I am relieved of the ranch too. I have asked that they keep my hands there. Of course, they can hire whoever they want, but my men know the place so well. I want them taken care of."

"Would be to that couple's advantage to keep them. They helped grow the place. Why replace them?"

"Exactly. Hope that works out."

"Yep," Sullivan agreed.

"Did you have a good day?"

"I did. I killed two men."

"That was good?"

"Yeah. They robbed the bank, shot a hole in the ceilin', and scared a lady half to death."

"I know it's a part of the job."

"It's the worst part. But like in the Rangers, I am paid to protect the citizens from violence, robbery, killin'. They could have surrendered. But they wanted to kill me. I am home tonight because I killed them. They were somebody's boys. I know that. But so am I, and I am somebody's husband who is glad to be home tonight."

"I'm glad you are too."

Chapter 5

The next morning, Sullivan reported to the office. He found Sheriff Clay Morrison waiting on him.

"Just the man I need to see," Morrison said.

"Here I am."

"I need you to go out to a small ranch just west of town. You'll find a man there named Short Delamont."

"Is he short?"

"He's tall. He is also trouble. He's been on a binge for months now. His wife died back in the Spring. He's also mean when he's drunk. He came into town last night, got drunk, shot up the saloon, and killed a man standing at the bar for no reason. He can't get over losing his wife, and he's been taking it out on the world. Everybody has given him some slack, a lot of slack. But I was afraid all along, it would eventually come to this. It did. Last night. I want you to bring him in."

"What if he don't want to come in?"

"That's between you and him. Just bring him in. He'll have to face justice. One way or another."

"How do I find his place?"

"Go about two mile out of town. West. You'll come to a little road that goes south. His place is down there about a quarter mile. On the right. Big barn. White house. Two big white oak trees."

"All right."

"Good luck."

Sullivan left the office, walking back home where he kept his horse in the barn and corral behind the big white house, he now called home.

Josephine saw him coming, and walked out to meet him.

"Where you off to?" she asked, when he came near.

"Got to go see a man."

"Oh, yeah."

"Yep."

"About what?"

"About a horse."

"What horse?"

"The one he's coming back to town on."

"Does he want to?"

"Not likely."

"How's he coming then?"

"Sittin' on him or laying across him."

"That bad?"

"That bad."

They walked on around to the barn. Sullivan saddled his horse.

"You know I can read you like a book," Josephine said.

"What page you on?"

"The one about danger."

"Turn the page."

"It's still like it was in a way. You still go out, and I don't know if you are coming back or not. You just don't go as far."

"I'm comin' back. And I'll be sittin' on my horse."

"You promise?"

"You can bet your life on it."

"I am. Be careful."

Sullivan mounted his horse, and said, "Always, in all ways."

He rode down the little hill, and turned west when he reached Fort Worth's main street.

Somehow things were different now. He had a different feeling. He felt like he had to be extra careful because of Josephine. He had never felt that way before. He had never thought much about that. He had never been careless. He had always fought to keep himself alive in the world. But in the midst of any battle, he had ever been in with anybody, any group, any enemy, he was never aware of thinking about how to save his own skin. He just functioned, did what he had to do, took the steps he had to take, carried out the mission.

What if he forgot to be that way now? What if, in trying to be careful, he became careless?

He could make a mistake, miss something, fail to concentrate.

When he reached the west end of town, he realized he had to quit thinking about all that. *Just do as you have always done,* he told himself. *You'll be all right that way.*

He had been along that road many times, going off to find or chase or kill Comanches or face Comancheros or any other variety of bad men. This day should be no different from any of those. He always came back, even when others did not.

Soon he came to the little road that went off to the south.

This is it, he thought.

Chapter 6

Sullivan rode down the little dusty road, looking far ahead in search of the little white house. Soon he saw it. He had that same feeling he often had when he knew he was facing trouble or was about to face it. A quickening of the pulse, a little jumpy stomach, breathing a little different. All of it warning him to get ready.

He knew he was as ready as he would ever be.

His eyes darted around, back and forth, searching the place for any movement, any sign of life. He saw no one, but he did see one lonely horse in the corral by the barn.

Short Delamont was at home.

Sullivan approached the house cautiously. When he came to the fence, he dismounted, and tied his horse to a fence post. He looked around.

"Short Delamont! I need to talk to you!"

"Go ahead! Talk!"

The voice came from the front door of the house. It was barely open.

"Why don't you come on out!"

"Why don't you come in! If ya think ya can!"

"That ain't a good idea!"

"Who are you?"

"Toombs Sullivan! Deputy Sheriff!"

"You the new guy?"

"That'd be me!"

"Didn't figger Sheriff Morrison had the nerve to come out here himself!"

"He's busy with important stuff!"

"Too bad! I don't want to kill the new guy!"

"I don't want you too neither!"

"I reckon not!"

"This can go two ways. Like I told a couple of men yesterday, there's the easy way, and then there's the other easy way!"

"What's the difference in easy and easy?"

"The first easy mean's you die right here right now! The other easy means you come go with me, and you get a fair trial! Maybe that man last night pulled his gun first! You go free, if that is true!"

"You promise?"

"I promise!"

"You promise I go free?"

"No! I promise you a fair trial!"

"You sure about that?"

"Do I look like a liar to you?"

"To me you look stupid!"

"Well, I ain't! Now, don't you be!"

"All right! I'm comin' out!"

"Leave yore gun in there!"

"Do I look stupid to you?"

"Can't tell yet!"

"I ain't. I'm comin'!"

"Put yore hands in the air!"

"All right! All right!"

"Keep comin' .... Keep comin' .... Now, put yore hands together."

Sullivan put the handcuffs on Short Delamont.

"Now, you stand right there while I saddle up yore horse for ya."

In a few minutes, Sullivan led Delamont's horse out of the corral and over to where he waited.

"Mount up, Delamont."

Delamont got up on his horse, and then looked back down at Sullivan.

"I'm gonna let you ride free, Delamont. But if you try anything, if you try to take off by yoreself, I will shoot you dead right on the spot."

"I understand."

"Good."

"I heard what you did to them two boys that robbed the bank. That's why I came on out."

Sullivan made no reply, as he mounted his horse. With his head, he motioned for Delamont to move out toward town.

As they headed for town, neither man said anything, Sullivan had nothing to say. Delamont was not in the mood for conversation.

When they stopped in front of the sheriff's office, they dismounted. Sullivan tied both horses to the rail.

He then opened the door, and led Delamont inside.

"Good work, Sullivan. Short, you are being charged with murder. You'll have a fair trial in a few days. Soon as the judge is ready."

"Ya gonna hang me?"

"Not for me to say. A jury will decide if you are guilty. The judge will decide the rest."

"Sounds wonderful. Got a drink?"

"I think that's what got you here. Take him on back, Sullivan."

Chapter 7

Everyone looked up suddenly when Judge Philo Donovan pounded his gavel the following Monday at nine o'clock. He was seated behind a table on the platform at the Baptist Church in Fort Worth. A new courthouse was being built, but it would be a while before it was ready. Many people thought it was strange to have court in a church. Judge Donovan knew they felt that way, and truth be told, he happened to agree. He knew it was on everyone's mind, at least most of them, so he felt compelled to make a comment about it.

"This court is now in session. It seems odd in a way to be here in this church. It is that unusual mixture of law and grace. I don't know, maybe they do go together.

Maybe it's like the bible. You got law in the first book, and then you got grace in the second book because no man can stand up against the law. Bumping into the law, he can only fall back on grace. That's what we got here today, I guess. I am the law. Grace said she could not be here today . . . . Order!" the judge said, as the crowded church was filled with laughter. "There'll be no more of that today. But anyhow, I will administer the law, and later God will handle the grace part. That is His job, not mine.

"So, we are here for the trial of Mister Julius Caesar Delamont. I don't know why they call you Short, Mister Delamont . . . . even though you ain't at all.

"Mister Delamont is charged with the murder of an innocent man last week. The man he killed was a local citizen of this town that we all knew and admired. His name was Alexander Wyatt. Mister Wyatt was a fine man. He leaves behind his dear wife, Edna, and five little children. Who will feed them now, I ask you?

"Well, anyhow, on with the proceedings. Mister Delamont, are you represented by counsel?"

Long, tall, skinny Jonothon Peale jumped up, and said, "Your Honor, I represent Mister Delamont."

"Fine. Sit down.

"And our prosecutor is Mister Daniel Vandiver.

"Mister Vandiver, are you ready to brings the charges against Mister Delmont?"

"I am, your Honor."

"Good. Let's hear it."

"Last Tuesday night at a local saloon, this man right over here I am pointing at, Mister Short Delamont, as he is known locally, willfully, purposefully, deliberately, pointed his pistol at the aforementioned Mister Alexander Wyatt and willfully, purposefully, and deliberately shot him down dead in that saloon. That is the case, and that is all there is to it. I have thirteen witnesses here today who will swear before God, and uh, our judge too, of course, that they saw him do it.

"Gentlemen of the jury, I will now call my first witness before you now at this time.

"Will Mister Highsmith Allgood please come and take the stand? That chair right over there."

Highsmith Allgood was sworn in.

Daniel Vandiver called all thirteen of his witnesses.

Each of them told the same story, just as Vandiver had laid it out for them.

"I was standing at the bar. Short was there, Short Delamont, and he just kept on drinking even though many of us tried to get him to stop. He kept on talking about his wife, and how she died in his arms. He got so drunk that he pulled out his gun, and shot it straight up. When Alex, Alexander Wyatt, tried to get him to stop, Short, Short Delamont, turned to his left where Wyatt, Alexander Wyatt, was standing, and shot him down dead. That's it."

"Would you please point to Mister Delamont . . . . Thank you. You may step down."

Twelve more witnesses came forward, with each one telling the same story.

After a break, Judge Donovon asked Lawyer Peale if he was ready to represent his client.

"Yes, your Honor," he replied.

"I call back to the stand Mister Highsmith Allgood."

Allgood was not happy with having to testify again. It was quite evident as he took the stand.

"Now, Mister Allgood, you testified that you saw Mister Delamont shoot and kill Mister Wyatt. Is that correct? Uh, you are still under oath."

"Yes."

"Mister Delamont had been drinking a lot, correct?"

"Yes."

"How much had you been drinking?"

"I don't know."

"Thank you. You may step down."

"Your Honor, I call to the stand the bartender, Mister Pots Fuller. I mean Charles Fuller."

Charles Fuller made his way to the stand, was sworn in, and sat down.

"Mister Fuller, you were behind the bar on the night in question, correct?"

"I was."

"Mister Delamont drank a lot. Correct?"

"Yes, he did."

"Did he drink more than the others?"

"Well . . . . I don't know."

"You served the drinks, correct?"

"I did."

"Did you serve more to Mister Delamont than the others?"

"I don't know."

"Sure, you know. You are under oath."

"Well, I guess they all drank about the same amount."

"It is said that Mister Delamont was drunk. Was he?"

"Yes."

"Were these thirteen witnesses also drunk?"

"Uh, I guess so."

"Thank you. You may step down.

"Your Honor, and gentlemen of the jury, they were all drunk. So how can any of them testify about what they saw when being drunk impairs the vision, the thinking, the perspective, the judgement of anyone in that state? These witnesses have no idea what happened that night. They just pointed to my client to protect themselves. Any one of them could have been the killer.

"Your Honor, I move this case be dismissed."

"Motion denied," Judge Donovon replied.

After another hour filled with speeches, motions, and objections, the case was handed over to the jury. They left the sanctuary, retiring to a back room. Ten minutes later they returned.

One of the men on the jury handed a sheet of paper to the judge.

Judge Donovon looked at it, and then told Short Delamont to rise.

When Short Delamont stood up, it was clear that he knew what was coming. His head was bowed down, his eyes were closed, but not closed tight enough to keep one lone and lonely tear from finding its way down his face all the way to his chin.

"Mister Delamont, you have been found guilty of the murder of Alexander Wyatt. I sentence you to death by hanging. That will be in the morning at nine o'clock.

This court is adjourned."

Chapter 8

"I have to stay at the jail tonight," Sullivan said to Josephine, as they ate supper together.

"The man on trial today?"

"Yes. Delamont. He'll hang in the morning."

"He killed a man in the saloon?"

"Yep. He was drunk. Shot a man down. But his lawyer said today, proved it, that all the witnesses were also drunk. That doesn't make it all right, of course."

After a pause for a moment, Sullivan said, "His wife died a few months back. The sorrow of it ate him alive. He stayed drunk a lot, I think. Couldn't live with it. Will die because of it."

"That is so sad."

"Sometime a man has to just make the best of something like that, and go on and live. Ya can't let it destroy ya. Guess nobody ever told him that."

"Did somebody tell you that . . . . when you found your wife and son dead after the war?"

"No. I just did it. I knew what I had to do. But I also ran from it, and that is how I wound up in Texas."

"I'm sorry you went through all that."

"Yeah. Well, I enjoyed the supper. Got to go on back now."

"All right. Be careful."

"You bet."

Sullivan walked down the hill from the house. A soft breeze came out of the west. It did little good, for it was a warm wind that blew even as the sun was setting over where the breeze came from.

He could see lamps being lit in the town, as he looked up and down the street.

When he went in the office, he found Sheriff Morrison sitting at his desk. Morrison looked up at him.

"Sullivan, Sadie is bringing over his last meal. Ought to be here at any moment now. I'll be here early to relieve ya. You don't have to leave of course, if ya want to see Delamont hang."

"Don't know why any man would want to see another man hang. But I'll go home and eat, and come back. I brought him in. I'll see him out."

"Good. I'm going on home now. Big day tomorrow. Have a good night."

"Thanks. You too," Sullivan replied, as Morrison walked to the door and left.

Sullivan walked over to the door that led to the back room where the cells were located. He went inside the room.

"How ya doin', Delamont?"

"How ya think. They gonna hang me in the morning."

"Not so good, I guess."

"Not so."

"Food will be here soon."

"Oh, wonderful. Got to keep my strength up, ya know. Got a big day tomorrow, and I got to be in good shape. Long journey, ya know."

"Yeah."

"Tell me, Deputy Sullivan, which journey is the longest, the one to heaven or the one to hell?"

"Couldn't say. Ain't been to neither one yet."

"Well, if you go to heaven, you send me a message about how long it took to get there. If ya don't, then I'll see you in hell. Then we'll both know about that journey. I think the journey to hell is the long one, and the journey to heaven is the short one. Snap. You go straight to it."

"I'm sorry it has come to this, Delamont."

"You're sorry!"

"You seem like a descent man."

"I was at one time. Quite descent."

"You were in the war, I guess?"

"Yes, I was. I was proud to fight for my country. I would have been even more proud if I could have died for my country. Then it would have been worthwhile, dying, ya know. Now, this . . . . this is a total waste of time. You were there too, I assume."

"I was, yep. Lucky to live through that. Most of my friends at the time did not."

"Which journey ya think they took, the short one or the long one?"

"I think they all took the short one."

"Then I hope ya get to meet up with them at the appointed time for you."

"Thanks. Me too."

"Deputy, you really think there is a heaven and a hell?"

"Mama said there is."

"Good enough for you, good enough for me."

"Your food is here."

Chapter 9

When Toombs Sullivan arrived back at the Tarrant County Jail, it looked like all five hundred residents of Fort Worth were there. Many of them had not ever seen a hanging, and they were anxious to find out what it was like.

A wagon was waiting in front of the building. There was a rope with a noose on it hanging from a crossbeam. There was not a tree suitable for hanging. There were no gallows like those in some Texas towns.

Sullivan pushed his way through the crowd. When he went inside, he found Sheriff Morrison looking out the window.

"Don't these people have anything better to do?" Morrison asked.

"Don't look like it, else they'd be doin' it, instead of bein' here."

"I reckon."

"How's our friend back there?"

"Not too good. I asked him earlier if the wanted me to get the preacher to come say a prayer for him. He said no, it was too late for even God to save him."

"How ya gonna do it, Clay?"

"I got a wagon out there. We'll stand him up in it. Tie his hands behind him. Put a bag over his head. And then I'll have the wagon driven away. The bag is to keep the men from screamin' and the women from faintin'. Anything can happen to a man when his hangs. It ain't a pretty site at all. I'd hate to have one of his eyes pop out, and hit a woman in the face. I'd be voted out of office next week."

"Guess so."

"Well, it's about time. Might as well go get'im."

The two of them went to the door leading to the back room. They opened the door, and saw Short Delamont sitting on the side of the bed, staring straight ahead.

"It's time, Short," said Morrison.

"I know it."

"You ready?"

"Ready? Would you be? How ya get ready? Ready to die? No man is ever ready to die."

"I know, Short. I'm sorry."

"Sorry? If you was sorry, you'd never a'sent yo Deputy after me. You would'a let it go."

"I couldn't have let it go."

"I know it."

Morrison unlocked the door to the cell.

"Turn around, Short. Put the cuffs on'im, Sullivan."

They led Delamont out of the cell, then over to the front door. There was a clamor outside, loud talking, laughing, the sounds of a joyful crowd celebrating some important holiday or event or special occasion.

Then the door was opened. A hush fell over the crowd like a blanket of snow suddenly falling from the sky. There was not a sound. It seemed that everyone there quit breathing all at the same time, one great gasp, all holding their breath in unison.

All eyes were fixed on Short Delamont. They did not see Sheriff Morrison and Deputy Sullivan. They may as well not have been there at all. Short Delamont could have been hanging himself for all practical purposes. They watched him come through the door, his eyes with that far away look, the expression on his face blank, his mouth half-way open.

The two lawmen helped him get up on the wagon. They showed him where to stand.

Sheriff Morrison placed the noose around his neck, looked at his face, and then spoke to him.

"Any last words you want to say, Short?"

"Huh?"

"Anything you want to say?"

"How about good-bye?"

"Good-bye, Short."

"I'll see ya there, Sheriff."

"Where's that?"

"Where we're both goin'."

"And . . . .?"

"And we'll both find out."

Sullivan placed a bag over Delamont's head so no one could see his face, the expression, the tongue hanging out, the bulging eyes, maybe one popping out.

Morrison and Sullivan hopped down off the wagon.

Morrison walked around to the front of the wagon, where the man driving it could see him.

The people in the crowd were still not breathing it seemed.

Morrison looked up at the driver of the wagon, and nodded his head slowly. The wagon pulled away.

There was a snap.

Then there was a collective gasp.

Then silence.

Then the people walked away.

Chapter 10

After the hanging, it was like air was let out of a bag. The town of Fort Worth settled back into its normal routines. Every man, woman, and child went about their business, their own business mostly.

What was true for the town, was also true for the sheriff's office. The long hot days seemed to drag by.

There were no arrests. Every person in town walked a straight line. No laws were broken. The people obeyed the laws, all of them.

"Is it often like this?" Sullivan asked Sheriff Morrison.

"No. Not always, but it seems to be after a hangin'. Maybe we ought to hang somebody ever now and then, just to keep the peace and calm."

"Not a bad idea."

"This won't last long. A cattle drive went through here about two, three months ago, headed up to Kansas. Abilene. Those cowboys get their money, and they come back down this way. They are determined to spend it all before they reach San Antonio, where they come from, those parts down there."

"I used to go to San Antonio. I started out as a Ranger down that way. Fought a lot of Indians down South. I'm glad to be out of the Indian business."

"Let's hope that is the case. I don't know which is worse, Sullivan, a wild Indian or a drunk cowboy."

"I would guess it is a toss up."

"Yeah," replied Morrison.

"I know one thing, if I don't move around, I'm gonna fall right to sleep, and fall right out of this chair."

"Yeah."

"Think I'll walk up the street a ways."

"Good."

Sullivan left the office, turned left, and headed up the boardwalk. He looked up and down the street. There were people out for sure, but no one seemed to be in a hurry.

He looked across the wide dirt street. It was the same on the other side.

Soon he came to Hart's Saloon on his left. He stopped to look in the swinging doors. There were a few men inside.

A couple of the young ladies were seated at tables where they were watching card games. The games were calm, slow, deliberate, with little interest even on the part of the players.

Sullivan went inside, and walked over to the bar. He leaned on it, and looked around.

"Deputy, I'm Pots Fuller. Charles, speaking properly, Charles Fuller. They just call me Pots. Why I don't rightly know. Haven't had a chance to meet ya yet."

"Oh, hello", Sullivan said, as he turned to face the bartender. "Toombs Sullivan. Glad to meet ya."

"And you too as well. Don't suppose you can have a drink on me while ya on duty?"

"Not hardly."

"I understand that," Pots Fuller said with a smile. "Maybe sometime later on."

"Yeah. I saw you at the trial."

"Oh, yeah, the trial. I hated that. Been kind of a friend of Delamont for a long time. Just glad they didn't ask me to testify against him. All of them really were drunk. Felt so bad for Short."

"Yep, I'm sure that was tough. Say, tell me about what happens in here when the cowboys come back down from Kansas."

"What doesn't happen is what ya mean, Deputy."

"Oh, yeah? Well, tell me all of it then."

"They come in here like the cows they been drivin' across all the long places where there is no water. Those old cows start smellin' it, and they'll break and stampede to get to it. They'll plunge right in, whether it's good water or bad. They don't care. They just want to drink it all.

"Those cowboys are like that. They come tearin' in here, rippin' and roarin' and snortin' like a herd of cattle that's been about to thirst to death. They get all tanked up, and ya never know what will happen. They'll start shootin' up the place, shoot out windows, mirrors, paintings on the walls. And sometime they'll shoot each other."

"Like Delamont."

"Yep, like Delamont."

"When do they get here?"

"Any day now," replied Pots Fuller. "Yep, they come tearing in here, ridin' wide open down the street, shootin' their pistols in the air. Oh, you'll know when they get here."

"How many?"

"Oh, I don't know. Let's just say a lot."

"That sounds like too many."

"It is. It is. Except for one thing. I sure do sell a lot of liquid products."

Chapter 11

Three days later, it happened. It was like a tornado sweeping into Fort Worth, right down the wide main street.

The dust flew up in the air. The sounds of horse's hooves filled the air. The gun-shots pierced the air. The yells and shouts and whoops shook the air.

Store-owners looked out their doors. Women ran through any door they saw open. At the bank, the newspaper office, and the telegraph office, doors slammed. At Hart's Saloon

and the undertaker's, the doors were wide open.

Sheriff Morrison and Deputy Sullivan were sitting in the sheriff's office. They had been there all day. It was like they were waiting, waiting in the quiet, the quiet that precedes the storm. The storm had finally arrived. It was five o'clock in the afternoon.

"What you just heard is the call to action," Morrison said. "Are you ready?"

"I am."

They walked out of the sheriff's office, and turned left, headed toward Hart's Saloon. By the time they got there, that first group of cowboys was already inside. The noise, the havoc, the earthquake, the storm, the tornado they were creating was already causing an upheaval in

Hart's Saloon that was only seen each year when the cowboys arrived.

When they stepped inside, all of the cowboys, all twenty-three of them, were gathered around the bar. Pots Fuller was pouring drinks as fast as he could. But it was not fast enough. Two of the girls who worked in the saloon were also pouring drinks. One of them was Masie Kilborn, and the other was Libby Lee. Also, part-time bartender Cedric Runnells was there helping out. But the four of them could not keep up with the demand.

"Here! Another!

"Bartender, pour me one!"

"Hey, Baby, fill my glass!"

"Over here! Hurry up! I need another!"

"Com'on! I got money, and I'm gonna drink it all right here, right now!"

Morrison and Sullivan stood there watching the spectacle as it unfolded, an exhibition of elbow exercise, a demonstration of the fine art of intoxication, a display of massive alcohol consumption, but no breaking of the law. They were there to enforce the law. No one had fired a weapon since the two lawmen had arrived. They would just wait and see.

Finally, it happened. One of the cowboys pulled out his pistol. There was a painting of a woman on the far wall behind the cowboys.

"Watch this!" he announced.

He turned around, and shot the wall three times, missing the painting each time.

"Well, well," he said mournfully.

"Let's grab him," Morrison said to Sullivan.

By the time they reached him, he had put his pistol back in his holster. He had turned back around, and was downing another drink.

Morrison taped him on the shoulder. He turned around.

"Mister," said Morrison, "you just fired your pistol into the store next door. You can't do that here."

"Slays, saves, says who?" he replied. "I'll flire, far, fire my gun anywhere I ca.. can, and want to."

"Not here."

"And who's gonna . . . . slop, stop me?"

Sullivan pulled out his pistol, and hit the man on top of his head. He quickly tumbled to the floor.

"Anybody else want to fire yore gun?" Sullivan asked.

Suddenly there was a calm, a stillness, a quiet that fell over the room.

"What's his name?" Morrison asked.

"That's Randy Arnold," one of the cowboys replied.

"We'll let him sleep it off tonight in the jail just down the street. One of you can come get him in the morning if ya like."

No one said anything.

"We'll be back here in a little bit. Let this be a warning to ya."

Still there was no response.

Morrison bent over, as he said, "Let's pick him up, and get him to the office."

They dragged Randy Arnold out of Hart's Saloon, and down to the office where they placed him in a cell in the back room, turned the key, and locked the door.

When they went back in the office, Morrison said, "All right, let's go get another. This could go on until midnight."

Chapter 12

The rowdy behavior of the cowboys in Hart's Saloon did indeed go on until midnight. Eight more were arrested before the saloon closed. They took their places in the jail cells.

The next morning, they were advised to watch their behavior during their hoped for exit from Fort Worth. By noon, all of that group had left town, headed South.

Before sundown, another wild group arrived in town.

This was a group of thirty-seven, led by their trail boss Texas Joe West.

As they arrived in Fort Worth, they kept up the tradition of galloping down the main street, shooting their pistols up in the air, yelling at women they saw, and generally disturbing the peace.

As soon as they came to a stop, they went storming into Hart's Saloon where the mayhem continued. That brought Sheriff Morrison and Deputy Sullivan out of the office. As they walked toward the saloon, they were met by trail boss Texas Joe West.

"Sheriff, how are ya?"

"Fine, Joe, and you?"

"I'm tired out, worn down, used up, dirty, hungry, low on patience, half angry, somewhat happy, and I need a drink. But first I wanted to come see you. How long has it been?"

"A good while for sure."

"For sure and for certain."

"This is our new deputy, Toombs Sullivan."

"Proud to meet ya, Sullivan."

"Likewise."

"Now, Sheriff, you know what my boys have been through. They been out a long time. They naturally are gonna blow off some steam. I'll do the best I can to keep the lid on."

"I know you will, Joe. But you know me well by now. If they get out of line, I'll have to rope'em up and bring'em in, ya know."

"I know. I know. But we'll work together on this. Right?"

"Right as rain, Joe."

"All right. Well, let's go have a drink."

The three men walked on up the boardwalk to Hart's. They turned, and went inside. When they stepped up to the bar, Joe West said, "Whiskey!"

He turned to Sheriff Morrison, and said, "You two?"

"No, Joe. We're om duty. Got to be able to drag your boys in."

"Sure."

By that time, Joe's drink was in front of him. He picked up the little glass, looked at it closely, then turned it up, and emptied it in one gulp.

"Yow. That's pretty fine whiskey."

"Only the best for you, Joe."

"Only the best. Hey, I'll have another!"

The drinking, card playing, talking, yelling, looking at the girls, went on until closing time at midnight. Only three of the cowboys fired their pistols at the ceiling. Only four got involved in fights. Only two threatened to kill somebody. Only one threw a chair across the room. Only one jumped over the bar, and tried to grab a bottle because the service was not fast enough. Each of those eleven cowboys were introduced to Sullivan's pistol as it struck them on the top of their heads. In each instance, they were dragged to the jail, and given free lodging for the night.

It was Sullivan's time to spend the night at the office, in order to watch over the jail and the inhabitants. They were all passed out, not from being struck over the head, but because of what they had consumed.

Realizing they were done and down for the night, Sullivan sat in the sheriff's chair, and leaned it back against the wall. In no time he was out for the night as well.

The bright light of the early morning sun came streaming through the front windows of the jail, waking Sullivan. He stood up, yawned, stretched, and went back to the cells.

"Awright, Cowboys! Time for you all to be up and out of here. The trail home awaits you."

The cowboys dragged themselves up and awake. When the cell doors were unlocked, they walked through them not remembering anything about the night before or how they got to the jail. They said nothing to Sullivan as he spoke to them.

"Good luck, Boys, and God-speed."

When they were all gone, Sullivan threw the keys to the cells on the sheriff's desk.

He left the office, knowing the sheriff would be coming in soon. He walked out across the wide dusty street, and headed up the little hill for home.

When he walked in the kitchen, Josephine was there making coffee, and getting ready to prepare breakfast for him.

"Mornin'" he said.

"Oh, good morning. How was it?"

"Constant."

"What?"

"It was constant."

"I thought you said Constance. That is the name of the woman who bought my ranch, Bill and Constance Giles."

"My wife was named Constance, ya know."

"Yes. Not many people have that name."

"No. Never heard it before, or since."

Chapter 13

A week later, Sullivan reported to the sheriff's office on Tuesday morning, just before eight o'clock. The sheriff was waiting on him.

"I got a job for ya, Sullivan. That Bill Giles that bought yore wife's ranch has reported cattle rustlers hit his place. They stole the major part of his herd. I want ya to go down there, and do what ya can."

"All right. I'll do what I can."

"You be careful. Those rustlers, people like that, they just as soon kill ya as to look at ya."

"Right. I have dealt with that kind before. The worst cattle thieves I ever faced were the Comanches. That is entirely different. At least these men, whoever they are, will not skin me alive. Will they?"

"Probably not. They don't have time for such."

"The Indians always had the time. They took the time. It was part of the fun for them."

"I can't imagine."

"No. You can't imagine what they do to people. The things I have seen are the stuff nightmares are made of, skinnin' people alive, cuttin' them open, scalpin' them. Men, women, and children. Nailin' a man to a barn door, then skinnin' him. Horrible. But we always dispensed justice Texas Ranger style whenever we could. And the

Comancheros were just about as bad. They didn't go for scalps and skinnin'. But they are ruthless killers. They deal with the Indians, ya know, buy their stolen cattle, and then sell them to the Army. It is the same cows the Army had. The Indians steal them, and then the Army buys them back from the Comancheros. Crazy. At least I ain't chasing them. I hope."

"Just watch it."

"I will."

Sullivan turned around, left the office, crossed the wide dusty street, and went back up the hill to get his horse.

Josephine saw him coming. She stepped outside, and met him as he approached the barn.

"You're back mighty early," she said.

"Yeah. That fella that bought yore ranch got hit by rustlers. They got most of the herd."

"My cows?"

"Yeah, Sheriff wants me to go down there, and see about it."

"They took my cows?"

"That's right."

"The varmints!"

"Yeah."

"I hope the boys are all right. Did he say if any of them were hurt?"

"Didn't say," Sullivan replied, as he walked on toward the barn, Josephine walking with him.

"They took my cows!"

"Seems like it."

"I'm going with you!"

"No, you're not."

"Why not?"

"This is official business. The sheriff is sending me. It is dangerous. And they are no longer your cows."

"Well, when you catch them, you give them the Sullivan treatment."

"That I will," he replied, as he threw his saddle onto his horse.

"You be real careful."

"Always."

"I love you."

"Love you as well."

"Are you going to kiss me goodbye?"

"Yep. But it ain't goodbye. It's just see ya a little later. I hope I won't be gone over night. But if I ain't back tonight, just know I'm fine. Ya know, it could get right involved. Don't worry."

Sullivan held Josephine in his arms, kissed her, and then let her go. He mounted his horse, tipped his hat, and rode down the hill to the street.

He left Fort Worth, and headed South down the trail he had followed so many times.

So, it's cattle rustlers now, he thought. He remembered all the things that had happened at that ranch. The times when, as a Texas Ranger, he had gone there chasing Comanches, as well as outlaws. He remembered friends who had died in those days in that part of Texas. And he recalled how Josephine had been kidnapped. Those were some difficult times, but he must have enjoyed it, loved it. He kept at it so long, and never gave any thought to giving up, to quitting.

Chapter 14

When Sullivan arrived at what had become the Giles ranch, he let his horse drink water, and then tied him to the rail. He looked around. There was no one there. No cows out in the upper pasture, no horses in the corral.

He walked over to see if the man's wife was there. She surely did not go off chasing cattle rustlers with the men.

He walked up to the front door, looked around some more, and then he knocked. He knocked a second time. The door was opened slowly.

"My God!" the woman gasped.

Sullivan said nothing. He could not speak. He was overcome with emotion. It was like facing a gun battle with robbers coming out of a bank, or a band of Comanches charging at him. His pulse quickened, his breathing became faster, his heart pounded. Then he managed to say one word slowly, haltingly, breathlessly.

"Constance."

They threw themselves into each other's arms. They held each other tightly for what was a few seconds, but seemed like days and months and years.

Neither of them could speak. All they could do was sob. Together they shook and trembled and sobbed some more.

The tears flowed down their faces, faces pressed together so that their tears mingled together and formed a little river of sorrow and regret and pain and heartache.

Each of them wanted to let go long enough to look at the other's face, but neither of them could let go. They wanted to speak, but neither of them had any words.

Finally, Sullivan said a few words.

"I thought you . . . . were . . . ."

"I thought you were . . . ."

"But I came home . . . . the graves. I found them."

"It was our boy, and, and a Yankee soldier."

"What?"

"The fighting came near our house. Our precious boy was struck by a stray bullet. The Yankee died in our front yard. Our boys buried both. Months earlier I had heard you were killed somewhere up in Virginia or some place. The story was unclear.

"I left there, and went to Atlanta where I had a cousin. I stayed with her until Sherman came, and took the city. We went west into Alabama where she had a friend. She took us in.

"When the war ended, I met Bill Giles. He came home to Andalusia where we were. We married, and came to Texas. We managed to buy a small ranch. Bill is really good at anything he does. We prospered. That's how we were able to buy this place.

"What in the world happened to you?" she asked.

"Let's go in, and sit down at the table."

They went through the house to the kitchen, both of them took a chair at the table.

"Well, when the war ended, I came home. When I got there, I looked around, expecting to find you, but I couldn't. Then I found two graves. It killed me, Constance. It killed me. I gathered a few things, some clothes. I burned the house."

"Oh, God," she said, as the tears and sobs came again.

"I went to Atlanta where I worked for months. Then I left to come out here.

"Soon as I stopped in the first town I came to, Marshall, I killed a man, two men, who were about to kill a Texas Ranger. The result being I became a Ranger myself.

"I could not get you out of my thinking. I had dreams about you where you were coming to me. I could not get you out of my mind and my heart. I was haunted by all that. But in the daytime, I had to concentrate on staying alive.

"I was stationed down in Austin. We fought Comanches all over that part of Texas, down beyond San Antonio, over toward the coast, all the way across to

Mexico. Then they sent me up here to Dallas. I spent several years chasing Indians and bandits everywhere.

"I had met a woman, the woman who owned this ranch, not long after I got up here. We wanted to get married. After several years of puttin' it off, we finally did. I took a job as a Deputy in Fort Worth, left the Rangers, she sold this place.

"And here we are, both married to different people because we both thought the other was dead and gone."

Constance began crying again. Sullivan reached across the table, and took her hand.

"What do we do?" she managed to ask.

"We're both married. And we're married illegally. Ya can't be married to but one person at a time. We're still married to each other."

"I know. What can we do? I still love you. I always have. I always will, Toombs."

"And I could never stop loving you."

"We must never let it be known who we are. As much as it hurts, we can never tell we are married to each other, that we still love each other. It would kill two people we also love. We cannot kill them with this."

"I know. I know that is true. I know it's right, the only right thing," he said.

"Yes. The right thing."

Toombs and Constance spent a couple of hours talking about the situation they were in. They held each other, shared forbidden kisses and words, and felt their hearts breaking all over again as they did when they first lost each other. Now they would lose each other a second time.

After two hours, Sullivan said, "I have to go. I hate leaving you. I don't want to leave, but I was sent here to try to help your husband with the stolen herd. I must. I must."

"I know. You have to. I know. But I will die. I will die from heartbreak. I can't stand it. I can't. I can't. Will I see you again?"

"Oh, I want us to meet again. But you know we can't. We can't do it. We have to let it lie where it is. There's no chance, no chance at all."

"Oh, God."

"I'm goin' now. I'm goin'. I'm goin' to the door. You stay here. Don't follow me."

Sullivan got up, and hurried through the house. He went to his horse, mounted up, and rode away quickly, never looking back.

Chapter 15

When Sullivan was out away from the house, he turned left around the corral, and went out across the upper pasture. Soon he came to where the herd had been, down near the lower creek. The trail was easy to follow, all those cows, all those horses. He would not have any trouble catching up with them, the rustlers and Giles and his men.

They were all headed South-west, down through country he knew so well. He would find them.

The trouble was he had no idea where the county ended. Frankly, he said to himself, he did not care.

There was another problem, a more serious one. They were almost a day ahead of him. How could he catch up?

One thing was clear. All of his training and experience as a Texas Ranger would come in handy. He knew just what to do, and was not afraid to do it.

On he rode, following the tracks which had torn a wide swarth in the earth. He paid no attention to the tracks really, just the torn-up ground. But then he saw something that caught his eye. He stopped, got down off his horse, knelt down, and looked at it closely.

He was shocked by what he saw. After looking at it, he began to notice others just like it.

His heart sank just a little. Why did it have to be this?

Mixed in with the tracks of cattle and Giles and his men, he saw the tracks of unshod ponies. Indians. Comanche Indians.

He thought he was through with all that. But now he was being plunged back into again.

That was beside the point now. What he had to focus on was getting to Giles, for he was in much bigger trouble than he thought he was. He thinks he is after cattle thieves, white men who are crooks who might just be scared away.

He was after bloodthirsty savages who would just as soon string him up and skin him as they would like to butcher a beef. In fact, they would enjoy him even more.

He had to ride all night, ride until he caught them. But he was without provisions, no food, no blankets, nothing to cook with, nothing. He was just supposed to go chase down a few rustlers. But if he was unprepared, it was his own fault. He knew better than to go off without thinking about what he might need if the search turned into something unexpected. It had.

He knew they would turn to the West, and not just head South-west. He had seen it before. They were headed to a rendezvous with Comancheros somewhere out there.

Most likely the Comanches had stopped for the night. They would not run the cattle without stopping for water and grazing for them. They would lose too many.

Hopefully Giles had also stopped to rest. He wondered what provisions they had brought with them. Maybe they had prepared themselves better than he had.

A full moon lit up the sky and the land, making his journey easier. He could see clearly the trail he was following.

When Sullivan came to a creek, he stopped to let his horse drink. He needed to walk around a little to get the blood flowing in his legs.

He heard the howl of a coyote not too far away, as well as the cries of the others in his pack as they raced to where he was.

There were other night sounds he had heard so many times before, sounds he had slept through without giving them any thought at all.

It was past midnight. Surely, he would catch up with them soon.

After five minutes of rest for him and his horse, he got back up on him. Away they went pursuing the herd, the Indians, Giles, his men.

Near dawn, Sullivan saw the flicker of a campfire in the distance.

A good way to get himself killed was to go riding in unannounced. He stopped, got down off his horse, and listened for a moment or two. He heard nothing. Were they all asleep with no guard?

He moved ahead slowly. He stopped short of the camp. He called out.

"Hello the camp!"

"I see ya, Mister," a voice answered out of the darkness. "I've been watching you for a while, hearing you longer than that."

"I'm Toombs Sullivan, Deputy Sheriff from Fort Worth."

"Out of your territory, aren't you? I'm Bill Giles?"

"Way out, Giles. Sheriff Morrison heard what happened to ya. He sent me to do what I could to help ya."

"I am glad for that. We need help. Come on to the fire. I put some coffee on."

In a couple of minutes, Giles poured both of them a cup of hot coffee.

"Giles, do you know who you are chasing?"

"Not at first, we didn't. But we soon found out. Makes me wish I had stayed at home."

"That goes for both of us."

Chapter 16

"So, what do you suggest we do?" Bill Giles asked.

"Well, you want your cattle back. I understand that. We'll get'em. But it's goin' to be tricky and dangerous.

Guess we need to think it through some. You got four men. With me and you, it's six against we don't know how many. I guess they would be the usual band, small band. They're the ones who steal cattle. Won't be the whole big tribe of'em. So, maybe there are fifteen to twenty I'd say."

"Three to one."

"If we're lucky."

"Can we handle that?"

"We can handle that."

"You sure?"

"No. You can never be sure about anything out here."

The men began to stir and wake up. They rubbed their eyes, shook their heads, stood up, brushed their hair back, and made their way to the coffee.

"Sullivan, it's you," said Luke Strothers.

"Still me."

"Heard you left the Rangers. So, what ya doin' out here?"

"Came to get you Boys out of trouble."

"You a Deputy now, I understand."

"That's right."

"Ain't you far out beyond yore territory?"

"I am. But we ain't gonna tell nobody about that. If we live through this."

"Love your optimism," said Lanky Reiley.

"Have to add a little realism, or you'd be too cocky when we go after those Comanches."

"Hey," Luke Strothers said, "how's Miss Josephine?"

"She's doin' well, considerin' she's married to me."

"Well, well."

"Sullivan, what are you doin' out here?" asked Stub Holden.

"I came to try to save yore hide."

"I thought you had better sense."

"I do. I was sent."

Jack Boy Watts was the last one to arrive at the fire and the coffee.

"Mornin', Sullivan. Did I hear you say you was goin' to save our hides?"

"You did, and I did. It remains to be seen."

"I don't like that kind of talk. I want certainty, confirmation, promises."

"I can deliver none of that, Jack. But we'll all do our best."

"Good enough, I reckon."

"Giles, just where is the herd?" Sullivan asked.

"Best we can tell, about two miles over that hill out there to the west."

"Who are your best shots?"

"I guess Strothers and Watts would be. Right, Boys?"

They all nodded their heads.

"And you?" Sullivan asked Giles.

"I'm pretty good."

"Here's the plan. It's late already. Sun'll be up after a while. Me and Holden and Reily are goin' to circle around the herd, and get on the other side. The three of you place yourselves where you can see real good. We'll stampede the herd back this way. The cows'll run over some of them if they are not awake yet. The rest will be charging after the herd. You Boys pick them off one by one. Try to have some good cover so the Indians won't shoot you. Questions? We'll start them toward you at sunup. Be ready."

All six men poured out what coffee they had not finished. They put out the fire. Then they saddled their horses. They mounted up.

Sullivan, Holden, and Reily went off to the north, in order to get around beyond the hill and behind the cattle.

Giles, Strothers, and Watts eased their way toward the hill. They stopped just before they reached the top of it.

They tied their horses where they would be out of the way. Giles and Strothers found cover on the right side. Watts went across over to the left side. They waited.

Giles looked up at the sky. It was still black. He could see all of the stars in the heavens. To the far east there was just the hint of a few gray streaks slowly moving westward. He saw them, and wondered how long.

Sullivan, Holden, and Reily were riding hard to the north, getting ready to turn west, and then circle back to the east once they got beyond the herd. They were racing against the sun. They had to get ready soon for the sun waits on no man.

Chapter 17

"Yah! Yah!"

Pistol shots rang out!

"Yah!"

Shots fired!

Cattle turned and ran!

Cattle stampeded!

"Yah! Yah!"

Shots fired!

Sullivan and Holden and Reily got the herd up and running, running wild!

The Indians were shocked!

Some managed to get on their ponies!

Some were run over by the herd!

Some grabbed their rifles!

The herd raced up over the little hill where Giles and Strothers and Watts were waiting!

The Indians, on their ponies, tried to turn the herd to their left!

Giles and Strothers and Watts began firing at the Indians!

Several Indians fell off their ponies, some of them into the wild stampede under the charging cattle!

Some of the Indians got around behind Giles and Strothers!

They fired at them!

Sullivan and Holden and Reily chased after the herd and the Indians!

They fired at the Indians!

The Indians suddenly began leaving, having given up the fight.

"Stay with the herd!" Sullivan yelled at Holden and Reily.

Watts joined them in the pursuit of the cattle.

Sullivan found Strothers kneeling down beside Giles.

He got off his horse, and walked over to where they were. Giles was lying on his back.

Strothers looked up, and said, "He's dead."

"What?"

"Dead, Sullivan. A few of them got around behind us. They missed me, but got him."

"Oh, God," Sullivan said.

Why this, he wondered? Why this?

It came to him in a flash. He could not be the one to go tell Constance about this. The emotions would be too deep, too raw, too real. He could not be there with her in that situation. That would not be good at all. He would help the boys get the herd back home, but he would go around the house, unseen by her. They would have to tell her. Yes, them. Just them.

"All right, let's get him up on his horse, and tie him down."

In a few minutes, they had Giles ready to go home.

"You go on now, and help with the herd. I'll bring Giles along, and try to catch up with y'all."

Strothers hopped up on his horse, and galloped off to catch the others and the herd.

Sullivan stood by the two horses, looking at dead Giles.

What a terrible thing to take place, he said to himself. And Constance. What will happen to her now? Josephine could handle the ranch when she had it. She was cut out for it. But not Constance. She was too delicate, too soft, too inexperienced. She would be overwhelmed by it.

He knew he must not think about those things. It was not his concern, not his business. It had to stay that way. He had to stay away from her and her problems.

The sun was fully up by then. Sullivan looked around at the dead Indians. They had killed nine of them. It looked like the cattle had killed another four or five. They had gone off their ponies, but maybe they were shot dead before being trampled into the dirt. Some had been run over before they could react at all. Whatever had happened, the Comanches had been hit hard, very hard.

Sullivan took the reins of Giles's horse, mounted up on his own horse, turned them, and began following the path of the herd and the men.

It was a long way back. Maybe they could get there before dark.

Soon Sullivan caught up with the herd. He pulled over to the side of it so Giles would not be completely covered in dust when they got him home.

Finally, as the sun began to sink down low in the west, beyond the hills and the horizon, they were within site of the ranch, the barn, the corral, and the house, a house that would soon feel very empty.

Sullivan pulled up alongside of Watts, and handed him the reins of Giles's horse.

"You take him on in, Watts. I have other things I have to go see about. Y'all explain what happened to him. And, uh, tell her I am very sorry. She'll know why."

Chapter 18

"How bad was it?" Josephine asked, when Sullivan came home late in the night. She was in bed.

"Bad enough. It was Comanches that stole the herd. I caught up with Giles and his men. Early the next morning, we stampeded the herd. Killed a lot of the Indians. Ran off the rest. But bad news. Giles was killed. Got the cows back."

"What?"

"He got shot during the raid."

"Oh, my goodness! What about his poor wife? How did she take it?"

"I don't know. I stopped by the ranch on the way. Saw her then. But not when we came back. I wanted to hurry on home. I let the boys tell her. Hope she'll be all right."

"I don't know how. Poor thing."

"Yeah."

"Are you hungry?"

"Starvin'."

"I'll get up, and fix you something."

"No. I'll do it. You stay in bed."

"I don't mind really."

Josephine got out of bed, and made her way to the kitchen. She fried a piece of ham, scrambled three eggs, and heated up the coffee.

Sullivan sat down at the table.

"You look worn out," Josephine said.

"Almost. Chasin' Indians again. I thought I was through with all that. Guess not. They just never seem to go away and stay away."

"I have something to tell you."

"Sounds serious."

"It is. I didn't want to tell you before you left. I didn't want you to have that on your mind while you were out there."

"All right. What is it?"

"We're going to have a baby."

"We're what?"

"A baby."

"That's wonderful," he replied, while quickly standing up. He rushed over, and hugged Josephine.

"When?"

"In the winter. Probably February."

"Well, this is great, just great."

"You've been through this before. I haven't."

"Oh, there's nothing to it."

"Not for you."

"You'll be fine."

"There's a midwife here in town. And the doctor is Doc Randall, James Randall. The midwife is Abigail Timms."

"You got it all lined up then."

"Did it while you were gone."

"Have you talked to them?"

"Yes. I just let them know, so they would have my name."

"Well, now, you need to take it easy."

"I don't know easy. I'll be fine. I feel real good. Really."

"We need to start gathering baby things. Baby clothes. And a crib. Things like that."

"We will. We have plenty of time."

"It'll be here before ya know it."

Sullivan drank some coffee, and began eating the meal Josephine had prepared for him. She poured herself a cup, and sat down at the table.

Sullivan thought about how his life had changed. He had spent years riding all over a good portion of Texas, without ever feeling at home anywhere. He had almost lived the life of a nomad. There was a constant battle out there in front of him. He ended one fight, then set off on another. He had killed so many, chased so many, fought so many, been attacked by so many that he, at times, had felt numb.

Now he had settled down in Fort Worth. There were still battles to be fought, but most of them would be local. He would probably not have many like the one from which he had just returned.

He was married, living in a fine house, a nice warm, dry place to sleep at night, good food every day, and life was good. He was being domesticated.

The final step in that process was before him. A baby would be the ultimate event in making him a more normal person with a more normal life.

He looked up at Josephine, smiled at her, then asked the important question.

"What are we goin' to name that little fella?"

"What makes you think it's a fella?"

Chapter 19

"Does the name Comanche Joe Storm mean anything to you?" Sheriff Morrison asked Sullivan.

"No. Can't say that it does."

"Your name apparently means something to him."

"How's that?"

"He was in the saloon the first night you were out of town. He said he was going to kill you, so I'm told."

"Why?"

"For the fun of it, he seemed to be saying. Seems like

you killed some of his kin somewhere along the way. He's a breed. Half Comanche. That's why he has that name."

"Comanche Joe, eh?"

"I don't care who you are or where ya go, our past always pursues us."

"I reckon so," Sullivan replied.

"It happened to me. It was in the war. I was a captain. Had in my unit some boys from down Austin way. Out in the country west of there. I sent one of them ahead to scout. His name was Johnny Hunt. He never came back. We found him the next day. It looked like maybe a sniper had shot him down.

"His brother Jimmy was irate, blamed me for his death. He knew he could not do anything to me. If he had, he would have been hanged. He knew it. One night in the dark, when there was nobody else around, he comes up to me, and says in a very low voice that he is goin' to get me when the war is over. If ya live through it, and if I live through it, and it seems doubtful for both of us at this time, I said.

"The rest of the war, he never said nothin' else to me at all. He kept his distance.

"I forgot all about what he said to me that night. I guess I thought it was just his reaction, a reaction of grief, sorrow, anger. It never dawned on me when the war was over, that he would actually follow up on his threat.

But he did.

"I had been back here two months, and went to work as the Deputy, the job you have. I was in the saloon one night, facing away from the door. I heard somebody call my name. I turned around, and saw him. I called his name, 'Jimmy', thinkin' it was a friendly visit. He pulled his pistol from under his coat, and shot my hat off my head. For some reason, he could not fire his again. Don't know why. But I could fire mine. I did. Dropped him right there where he stood.

"Men'll hold a grudge for a long time. It takes hold of them. It becomes their reason for livin'. They think about nothin' else. They have got to see it through. To the end. Often, it is their end.

"Seems to me this Comanche Joe Storm has that kind of grudge against you. You killed somebody close to him."

"Could he be arrested for threatenin' a law enforcement officer?"

"If I had heard him say that. I wasn't there. I heard about it later. I don't even know what he looks like. Just heard of him before. He's one of these mysterious characters. People know of him, but nobody knows him. He never comes around that anybody knows about it. Maybe on the other hand, he does come around.

"The story I got was that he said it in the saloon, but I talked to several of the men who were in there that night. None of them said they saw him, or heard him say it. But they said somebody said he said it. Maybe he was not there at all. Pots Fuller said there was nobody new there that he did not know. Just the same old crowd. It's really strange."

"A rumor can't start itself," Sullivan responded. "Seems like somebody got it there, and got it started. For him."

"Yeah. We'd best be real careful, be on the lookout for anybody new."

"This kind will never be seen by us. We won't know he's here. He'll come out of the dark unseen, unheard, when we are not expecting him. I have dealt with this kind before. He probably has enough Comanche in him to just be deadly silent and deadly."

"We'll be on the alert from now on," Morrison said.

"On the brighter side, I have some good news. We're gonna have a baby."

"Ain't that the way? Bad news, and then good news at the same time."

"I guess they sort of go together," Sullivan replied. "There's a fight goin' on between them. One seems to get the upper hand, and then the other one reaches out, and take his enemy by the throat. Who wins in the end depends on who had the last chance before the end got there."

Chapter 20

Comanche Joe Storm was the son of Joseph Roundtree Storm, a man who came to Texas from Louisiana about 1840. He became a hunter, trapper, scout, cattleman, and farmer.

Soon after he arrived, he became a friend of a Comanche band, often supplying them with meat. He married the daughter of a chief. Her name was Burning Flower. Not long after that, they had a baby. He was named after his father.

Like his father, Comanche Joe chose to live in both

worlds. It was whites who called him Comanche Joe. The Indians called him Man Who Hunts By Night.

He grew up to be taller than his father, over six feet tall. He was strong as well as fast of foot, and also on horseback. Both his father and the Indians trained him to hunt, track, fight, defend himself, and kill, both animals and men.

When the Civil War began, he refused to go into any Texas unit, even though he was required to sign up. He said it was not his fight. He hid out with the Comanches. This meant he traveled with them, hunted with them, stole cattle with them, and killed whites and others with them.

After the war, he left the Comanches, and he left his two young wives and their children. This did not endear him to some of the Indians, and especially the fathers of his wives. They were Running Horse and Big Tall Tree. But most Comanches felt he was a great warrior, a man possessed with wonderful powers and big medicine.

Leaving the Comanches set him off on a career of killing, robbing banks and stagecoaches, as well as individuals wherever he found them. He was also a gun for hire. He would kill any man for a price. Any person who had been offended, wronged, or who had a grudge with another man could hire Comanche Joe to murder his enemy. Yet, no one knew how to get in touch with him, how to find him, how to employ him.

Since he was hardly ever seen by anyone, except his victims, many people said he was more reputation than reality. But the reality was people were found dead who had been robbed. They were always killed in Indian ways, horrible ways.

Attacking and robbing individuals usually took place at night, hence the Indian name Man Who Hunts By Night, a tactic he first used in killing animals for the Indians.

Often when a person was found dead on a morning, he was suspected as the one who committed the murder.

He ranged far and wide, traveling all over the northern half of Texas.

Oddly enough, he had many friends it was believed. The Indians were always willing to take him in and hide him out. He had friends among many who were described as outlaws. He was one of them. Even among them, he was feared because of his sometime erratic behavior, his skill in the art of killing, and his lack of any feeling about anything human or animal. Then there were the people who were not outlaws, but were against the law, resenting any kind of civil authority.

For all of the above, he was a provider of whatever they needed. If a family was in need of food, and he heard about it, they just might find a dear or even someone's dead cow lying at their back door when they first got up.

Comanche Joe Storm was not just a kindhearted man who looked after people and their needs. He always had an ulterior motive behind these acts of generosity.

He just might need a favor someday from one of them, a place to hide, a warm meal on a cold night, or some other favor.

What did he look like? How would anyone know him if they saw him? The descriptions varied.

He was tall and thin, with black hair, and a black beard. He was short and hefty, solid, strong, blond hair and blue eyes, odd for someone who was half-Indian. He was medium build, medium height, and walked with a limp, the result of a fight with a bear. He was blind in one eye, and wore a patch over the left one. He had lost that eye at the Alamo, even though the battle occurred before he was born. He rode a black horse, a white horse, a pinto, an Indian pony. He carried two pistols, and one pistol, and two knives and one knife. He used a shotgun, 12 gauge, 10 gauge, 8 gauge, and 20 gauge. He never used anything but a Winchester rifle. He wore a black hat, a white hat, a Mexican style hat, and no hat at all. He wore black boots, brown boots, no boots, only moccasins. He always wore a black shirt, a red shirt, a blue shirt, a white shirt, and never changed from that color. His pants were black, brown, tan, leather. He was married to two Comanche women, except when he was married to one white woman who lived in San Antonio or Dallas or New Orleans or San Francisco. He had two children or three children or twelve children or no children.

Everybody knew him, but nobody knew him. Everybody had seen him at least once, but those who really had seen him did not live to tell about it.

This was Comanche Joe Storm. Or was it?

Chapter 21

Toombs Sullivan woke up as the first streaks of light raced across the eastern sky. He slipped out of bed, slipped on his pants, slipped on his boots, and slipped out of the room, hoping he would not wake up Josephine. He made his way through the house, headed out the back door for the outhouse. When he opened the door that led to the little back porch, he found a dead mountain lion lying on the back steps.

He heard footsteps coming up behind him. Josephine placed her hands on the back of his shoulders, as she looked around him.

"What in the world?" she asked astonishingly.

"A dead lion."

"How did it get here?"

"I don't know. I wish I did."

"Did somebody shoot it somewhere, and it just came here to die?"

"I doubt it. I think somebody shot it somewhere, and then they brought it here already dead."

"Why? For what reason?"

"I got no idea."

"I'll get dressed, and fix you some breakfast."

"Thanks. I'll try to figure out what to do with this thing."

As they ate breakfast, Josephine asked Toombs about the lion.

"Do you know yet what you are going to do with our visitor?"

"I think I'll put him up on my horse behind me, and take him off somewhere and dump him. Pass the sugar. Thanks. That way the varmints will have a good meal.

Butter, please. Thanks. And the buzzards. Good coffee."

"Need this knife?"

"Yeah, thanks. Still a mystery to me."

"Maybe there is a reason for it," Josephine suggested, after thinking for a moment.

"There's a reason for everything. But what?"

"We'll have to find that out."

Later that morning, when Sullivan walked down the hill toward the main street. He was still puzzled about the dead lion. *There must be somebody in this town who knows something about this*, he thought. *Somebody must have seen something. But then it must have been done in the middle of the night, or early morning, all in the dark.*

When he arrived at the office, he told the sheriff about the lion.

"What? I never heard of such a thing! What in the world?" Sheriff Morrison exclaimed.

"Me neither. I don't know what to make of it."

"It was done for a reason. That's for sure. Crazy things like that don't just happen randomly. Maybe somebody is tryin' to tell you somethin'."

"I think so. That's what I told Josephine. There's some reason for this. I just don't know what the message is. What does a mountain lion have to do with anything I ever did."

"I don't know. Maybe we'll figger it out. How is she by the way?"

"She's doing well. Seems to be all right."

"Good. Good. By the way after I left the saloon last night, a fella acted up, caused some problems. I was out walking through town, just doin' the rounds. It was young Ben Priest. They live up north of town. By the time I came back around he was gone. I want you to go talk to Pots. Find out what happened. Then go see the boy and his dad. Maybe just give'em a kind of warning. I bet his dad don't know nothin' about what happened. I don't know them very well, but as always be careful. Place is easy to find. Take the north road, big house up on a hill, couple of big trees in the front of it."

"Sure. I'll go on now."

Sullivan left the office, and walked down to the saloon. When he got there, he saw Pots Fuller sweeping out the place.

"Mornin', Mister Fuller."

"Oh, hey, Deputy. I didn't know you was talkin' to me at first. Mister Fuller's been dead twenty year now. How are ya? Just call me Pots like everybody else. They all say I have gone to pot, so Pots I am."

"All right, Pots. I understand you had a little trouble last night."

"We did, for a few minutes there."

"What happened?"

"It was that Priest boy, Ben. I said that boy. There's two of them. Ben is the mean one. He's about, I don't know, early twenties. The other is Bob, a little older. He ain't right in the head. They don't let him come to town. Ben got about half drunk, started a fight, broke a chair, said he was gonna kill a man, but he didn't. He left. But I don't like him bein' in here like that."

"The sheriff has asked me to go up, and have a talk with him and his dad."

"Oh, my goodness. You be real careful. They're all crazy. Real careful, I mean. Yeah, real crazy."

"I will. Say, you know anyone around here who likes to hunt mountain lions?"

"No. Why?"

"Just wonderin'."

Chapter 22

As Sullivan rode out of Fort Worth, headed north, he had the lion tied and draped over his horse, just behind him.

He wondered why he was told by both Sheriff Morrison and Pots to be careful. Pots even said be real careful. He said those people were crazy, real crazy.

He was not concerned about those remarks, until he got out of town, and thought about them some more.

Now he wondered if he was about to get into something he would just as soon avoid.

A mile out of town, he pulled off the road, and went down into a wooded area. He got off his horse, untied the lion, and laid him down in a place he would easily be seen by any animal or bird that wanted him.

Based on what he thought he was told, he had about three or four miles to go.

He kept thinking about these people he was going to see. Would they be armed? Would they shoot first, and then ask who are you?

Soon the house came into view. There it was, off to his right, sitting on the hill, just as he was told. There were a few chickens running around in the yard. A lazy looking hound was lying on the porch, enjoying a nap it appeared.

The barn was beside and to the right of the house. It was not in very good shape. There were two wide doors leading to the inside, one of them barely hanging on, the one on the right. In the corral were four horses.

"Hold it rat thar!" a voice called out, as Sullivan approached the house. He could not tell where it came from, the house or the barn.

Suddenly a man appeared at the far left corner of the house. He was an older man. Must be the father, Sullivan thought.

"What be yore business?"

"Can I come on up, and get off my horse?"

"I said, what be yore business?"

"I'm Toombs Sullivan, Deputy Sheriff."

"So?"

"Sheriff Morrison sent me up here to talk with you."

"With, to, or at?"

"Certainly not at. Probably not to. Most likely with."

"Come on up . . . . Get down. Keep yore hands whar I can see'em."

Sullivan moved closer to the house, and dismounted slowly, very slowly.

The man lowered the shotgun as he came on around the corner of the house, and walked toward Sullivan.

"So, the sheriff sent ya up here?"

"That's right."

"What fer?"

"You have a son named Ben?"

"Yep. And Bob too."

"Ben was in the saloon."

"I'm Big Bob."

"Nice to meet ya, Bob."

"Go on."

"He drank a little too much, I understand."

"And?"

"He said he was goin' to kill a man. Caused some trouble. Broke a chair."

"So?"

"We'd like for you to speak to him about it."

"You speak to him about it. He's come up behind ya, Deputy."

Sullivan looked back, and saw who he assumed was Ben standing behind him, about thirty feet away, holding a shotgun.

"Let me kill'im, Pa?"

"Naw! Let me do it, Pa!"

Suddenly the front door of the house burst open. There stood another young man, Little Bob, Sullivan imagined. He was also holding a shotgun.

All three shotguns aimed at him were double-barreled, probably twelve gauge, he thought. He did not stand a chance.

"All right, Ben, I'll speak with you. Don't come into town, and say you're going to kill a man in the saloon. Watch how much ya drink. You owe some money to Pots Fuller for a broken chair. Next episode like that will wind you up in jail."

"Want me to kill'im now, Pa?"

"You blink your eyes one time, and I will put a bullet between them. You and them may kill me, but you will go first. 'Bout two minutes you will wake up in hell. You think it's hot here? You ain't seen nothin' yet. Now make up yore mind, Sonny Boy."

There was a moment of silence when no one blinked, not even Sullivan. Then Big Bob spoke.

"You Boys lower yore guns. Let'im go. Now Deputy, ya made ya point. Now you git on back to town."

"You remember the point I made, Big Bob, Little Bob, and Little Ben."

Sullivan got on his horse, backed him up several yards, then turned him around. He headed back to the road, turned left, and breathed a sigh of relief, happy no one had called his bluff.

Chapter 23

Sullivan returned to the sheriff's office shortly before noon. When he walked in, he saw Sheriff Morrison looking at some wanted posters. He looked up at Sullivan.

"How did it go?" Morrison asked.

"I'm back alive."

"That says everything."

"Rough bunch of people."

"The worst kind. Well, almost the worst. There's always

somebody else who is worse. Take this one for example," Morrison said, as he tossed a wanted poster over toward Sullivan.

"Who's this?" Sullivan asked. He picked the poster up off the desk, looking at it closely.

"Name's Butch Coker. He killed a man in Dallas over a card game last night. Got a telegram saying he might be coming this way. He's wanted for bank robbery, murder, theft, and who knows what else he's done. Lived a life of crime before the war as a young man, and since he got back from the war. He's become even worse now. Just petty stuff as a kid."

"Nobody in Dallas recognized him last night, yesterday? He just walked in like a law-abiding citizen?"

"I guess the right person didn't see him."

"He's got a lot of guts, just walking around any old place."

"Keep your eyes open for him. You take this side of the street. I'll go across. Ask everybody you see if they know him, about him, seen him? Take that poster with you. Show the picture. I've got another."

"Sure."

Sulivan left the office, turned left, and went down the boardwalk. He came to Hart's Saloon. He went inside, and found Pots Fuller standing behind the bar. He was wiping it with a small white towel or rag.

"Hello, Deputy."

"Pots."

Sullivan laid the poster down on the counter. He turned it around so Pots could see the face.

"Ever seen this man before? Ever come in here?"

"Uh, yeah. I've seen him. He's been in here. Been a while. Can't remember when. Butch. Butch Coker. Wanted. No surprise to me. Glad you made it back, by the way."

"So, you know about him?"

"Just know he got a bad reputation. That's all."

"Was he wanted then, when he was in here?"

"Oh, I don't know. I don't remember when it was, last year, year before, year before. Who knows? I don't."

"But you knew he had a bad reputation?"

"Sure. Everybody knew that. He just as soon kill ya as to look at ya. That's why he got along so well with everybody. Nobody would say any cross word to him."

"We think he might be comin' this way. Killed a man in Dallas. If ya see him, or hear anything about him bein' around, let me know. Find me. Send someone to find me."

"You bet."

Sullivan left the saloon. He met a number of people on the boardwalk, went in every store he came to, showed the poster to every person he met, and no one knew anything at all. They had never seen him, had never heard of him, knew nothing about him. They said. They all said. They all said the same kind of thing.

"Nope, never heard of him."

"Never seen him."

"Looks mean. Don't know him or of him."

"Never saw that man at all."

"Naw. Don't recognize him."

"Him? Nope."

A little over an hour later, Sullivan and Morrison met back at the office.

"It seems a little odd to me," Morrison remarked. "He's been around here. I even saw him at least once. He wasn't wanted at the time. At least, no poster had been sent here. He was probably wanted somewhere by somebody for something, but we didn't know it. I don't remember when it was."

"Maybe it's not so odd," Sullivan replied, after thinking a moment. "People don't want to get involved. They got enough to be afraid of already. Why would they want to be the one who points the finger at him, and then have him find it out? That's a real easy way to get yoreself killed."

"It'll be on us, Sullivan, if he comes here."

"It always is. That's what we get paid for."

Chapter 24

The next morning, Sullivan was again up at dawn. He slipped through the house, headed for the outhouse. When he opened the back door, he was shocked at what he saw. There lying on the steps was a dead eagle.

He looked down at the bird, then looked all around the back part of the yard. He stepped over the eagle carefully, and began looking all over the ground for tracks. He saw none, not one.

When he went back inside, he built a fire in the stove. Then he put the coffee on to boil.

Soon, Josephine came into the kitchen. She spoke first.

"Good morning."

"I don't know about that."

"What? What do you mean?"

"There's a dead eagle on the steps out there."

"Not again?"

"Again."

"What in the world?"

"I wish I knew."

"I want to look at him."

"Right. Come on out."

Together they went to the back door. Sullivan opened it.

"My goodness," she said. "What a beautiful creature. Such a waste."

"Yeah. After I eat, I'll take'im on out back, and dispose of'im."

They went back inside, poured some coffee, and Josephine prepared breakfast.

When they sat down to eat, she just looked at her plate.

"What is it?" Sullivan asked.

"I can't eat this."

"Sick again?"

"Every morning for a little while. It'll pass. I'll be fine. I'll eat this later."

"Sorry."

"Don't be sorry. It means I am where I should be in this, and everything is fine. It'll stop in a few weeks."

"I sure hope so."

After he was through eating breakfast, Sullivan got dressed, and went to the office, arriving there a good bit before eight o'clock.

"Mornin'," Sheriff Morrison said, as Sullivan walked in through the door.

"Mornin'."

"Any visitors during the night?"

"Matter of fact, yeah. This time, a dead eagle on the back steps."

"You're not jokin', are you?"

"Not in the least bit."

"My goodness. I don't know what to say."

"I don't know what to think, say, or do."

"Guess not. All you can do is wait and see. Unless, of course, you want to sit up all night, and wait on whoever this is who's doin' it."

"That ain't a bad idea. It may come to that."

"Say, a kid came in here while ago. Said he had a message for you. Pots Fuller wants to see ya. Has somethin' to tell ya."

"Well, maybe it's important. I'll go see what it is."

Sullivan left the office, and went to see Fuller in the saloon. When he walked in, Pots Fuller was sweeping the floor.

"Deputy, how are ya today?"

"Fine. And you?"

"I'm doin' well. I got something for you. Come over here, and sit down."

They went to a table near the back wall, both taking a seat.

"An old friend of mine came in here last night, Tom Johnson. Haven't seen him in I don't know how long. He just never comes around. He don't drink alcohol, so why come here. Right?

"Well, Sir, we were talking, and I happen to mention how Butch Coker might be coming this way, and did he know him? He told me something I never knew, never heard before.

Butch Coker is the brother of Mable Lee Priest, wife of Bob, mother of those two boys.

"Of course, he's coming this way. He's coming home, seeking refuge. He'll hold up there, and think nobody will ever know about it."

"Your friend is sure about this?"

"I reckon he is. Said he grew up with Butch and Mable Lee and Bob. He wasn't Butch back then when they were young. He was Elroy Ludwick Coker."

"Guess he didn't like his name," Sullivan commented.

"They all came here from Mississippi together about the year eighteen forty-five, fifty. The Cokers, the Priests, the Johnsons, they all came together. Guess it was only natural that Mable Lee and Bob paired up, he said. He'd always had his eye on Mable Lee, but he was shy, shy too long he said. Missed his chance."

"Thanks for this. Very important, I better go inform the sheriff."

"Yeah. I can see he would want to know."

Chapter 25

Sullivan did not sleep well that night. He slept very little, waking up at least five times that he could remember. Then he laid awake for almost an hour, waiting for the sun to come up. Finally, mercifully, the sun peeped up timidly over the distant hills beyond the eastern edge of town. The darkness had been chased away, scampering off toward the western horizons.

He kept thinking about his conversation with the sheriff about Butch Coker, and the revelation of his local family ties. They had talked about how everything had suddenly become more complicated. What could they do other than wait until they saw him or heard that he had been seen? And where he had been seen?

Sullivan got out of bed, and headed for the back door.

He stood there for a moment, dreading opening it, not knowing what he would find this time.

Then he opened it, and found nothing. There was no dead animal or bird on the steps. He breathed a sigh of relief.

He walked out across the yard to the outhouse. He went inside, closed the door, and sat down.

Chips of wood and splinters flew all over the inside!

All over him they flew!

He heard gunshots ringing out!

He hit the floor quickly!

He laid flat down!

Five quick shots, the bullets tearing through the outhouse just above him!

Then there was nothing, nothing but silence.

The silence seemed loud and haunting.

He did not dare move.

"Toombs!"

Josephine was calling out to him from the back door.

Now she was in danger!

He jumped up, pulled his pants up, and looked out the door.

There was no one there but a frantic Josephine running toward him.

"What happened? What happened? Are you all right?" he heard her calling out.

He ran out toward her, shouting, "Back inside! Quick!

Get down," he said, as they reached the door, rushing inside.

He yanked his pistol from the little table by the door where he always kept it.

"What is it?" she cried out.

"I don't know except that somebody just tried to kill me."

"What? Why?"

"I'm a lawman, that's why. It just happens. Happened before. Will happen again."

"What now?"

"He's gone now, whoever it was."

"Will he come back?"

"I don't know. Since he didn't get me this time, he'll probably try it again."

"What can you do? How can you stop it?"

"Kill him first is all I can do. Whoever it is."

"How can you know? How can you find out?"

"I have no idea. Just wait on him, I guess. It's the only thing I can do."

Then there was silence, as they sat on the floor by the door with their backs to it. Nothing could be heard but their breathing. Sullivan looked at Josephine, smiled, and put his left hand on the right side of her face. He brushed her hair back off from across her eyes.

"You'd better make some coffee, and fix me some breakfast. I got to go to work. The day waits for no man, they say."

"You're not kidding me, are you?"

"Nope. I go to work every day, don't ya know?"

"Yes, but . . . ."

"No buts. Breakfast. Coffee. You."

"Fine. Have it your way. But if you wind up dead, don't say I didn't try to tell you differently."

"I won't say a word. I promise."

"I guess not."

"What I have to do is report this to the sheriff. He needs to know his best and most important and most valuable deputy almost got killed."

"You are his only deputy."

"Right."

Sullivan finished dressing, while Josephine prepared breakfast.

They ate slowly, talked a little, looked at each other a lot, both of them knowing how close he had come to being killed, how close she had come to being a widow. Again.

Chapter 26

"So, ya got no idea who it might have been?" Sheriff Morrison asked.

"Don't have a clue. Must have been my friend, the animal killer. But I thought about something walking down here. All those shots were high. He wasn't tryin' to kill me. He was tryin' to miss."

"That makes me think it was the animal killer just sending you a message. He's taunting you for some reason.

But what could that be?"

"If I knew that, I would know who it is."

"I hate to change the subject. But I been thinking. We can't just sit here and wait on a man to be seen by somebody, when he has gone to his family to hide, and not be seen by anybody. We got to go up there, see if he's there, and bring him in."

"I agree."

"Then go get yore horse. Meet me in the street."

When Sullivan got home, he whistled as he walked by the house, headed for the barn. Josephine heard him, and came out the back door.

"What are you doing?"

"Gettin' my horse."

"I figured that," she said, as she followed him. "So where are you going?"

"After a bad man."

"Who?"

"He's the brother of that Priest woman."

"What did he do?"

"Bad stuff. He's a bad man."

"Will you be gone long?"

"I sure hope not. If I ain't here by supper, it means I ain't comin' back at all."

"I wish you wouldn't tease me."

"I ain't teasing ya. Love ya, woman."

"I love you."

"Well, if you do, then do me a favor."

"What's that?"

"Go get my rifle for me."

As Josephine turned around to go back to the house, Sullivan added to his request.

"And bring the Sharps with ya as well."

"That serious, eh?" she replied.

"Yep. May be that serious. I want to be prepared, just in case."

As Sullivan finished getting his horse ready, he looked up and saw Josephine coming back with the two rifles, the Winchester in one hand and the Sharps in the other.

He took them from her, and placed the Winchester on the right side of the horse and the Sharps on the left.

He pulled out his pistol, making sure it was fully loaded.

"Thanks," he said to Josephine.

"Be careful. Careful. Come back."

"I will. I always come back."

He held her tight, kissed her, and then climbed up on his horse. He gave her one last look. Then he rode down the hill to the wide, dusty main street.

There he found Sheriff Morrison waiting for him.

"I see ya got the Sharps."

"I do."

"Good idea. Might need that. Depending."

"Depending."

"Let's go."

They rode out of town, headed north, neither of them saying anything for a while.

"How ya want to go about this?" Morrison finally asked.

"I don't know. What ya think?"

"Maybe one of us goes in, and the other covers."

"Good," Sullivan answered.

"You got the big gun. Seems like you'd be the one to cover."

"I'll cover."

"I'll go in."

"Right."

"Maybe they'll be in a good mood."

"Wrong."

"You think not."

"They'll be in bad mood."

"That ain't good."

"It won't be good for them. They better behave. All I got to say," Sullivan replied.

"That's enough then."

Chapter 27

When they drew near the house on the little hill, they stopped for a moment to look around.

"How many horses did they have when you were here?" Morrison asked.

"Four. I think."

"There's five now."

"They got company."

"Wonder who?"

"I think we know."

"Well, this ain't gettin' it done. Where ya gonna be?"

"There's that little rise on the side of the hill just to the right over there. I think I could get a good shot of them everywhere except over on the left side of the house. One of them will come around that corner. They'll all likely have shotguns except for Butch. I'm thinking he'll have a rifle or maybe just his pistol."

"Not much cover for ya."

"There's that boulder about a foot high. I can lie down behind it, prop my rifle, and have a little cover."

"Good. Here we go. I'll go slow, and give ya time to get up there."

While Sullivan tied his horse to the limb of a small tree, and took both of his long guns with him as he hurried up the hill, Morrison slowly rode toward the house.

Morrison stopped about forty yards from the front of the house.

"Hello the house!"

"Hello yoreself!" a voice replied from the barn.

Sullivan was surprised by that, as was Morrison. One in the barn, one around the left corner, two more somewhere else, Sullivan was thinking.

"Need to talk with Butch!"

"Talk then!"

"Need him to come out so I can see him!"

"You say you want to see him?"

"That's right!"

"Well then, go right in. He's waitin' on ya!"

"That won't work! I got to see him first!"

"First? Before what?"

"Before I kill him!"

A shot rang out from the barn!

Morrison dove off his horse, rolled on the ground, got up, and ran to the outhouse off to the left side of the house!

Another shot!

A different sound!

Big Bob Priest fell out of the upper floor of the barn!

That's one down, Sullivan said to himself.

A shotgun blast!

Part of the outhouse door flew through the air!

Sullivan could not see that shooter.

Morrison lay flat on the ground as he crawled to where he could see around the front of the outhouse.

Another blast!

Dirt flew up in the air in front of Morrison!

He ain't a very good shot, not even with that scatter-gun, Morrison said to himself.

Then he saw him coming toward him, reloading. It was Little Bob.

Morrison fired twice with his pistol!

Little Bob Priest hit the ground hard!

Two down, two to go, Morrison thought.

Sullivan put the Sharps down, picked up his Winchester, and ran for the barn.

From the barn, Sullivan had a good view of the front of the house, and everywhere on that right side of it.

Morrison was still beside the outhouse, only crouched down on one knee. He waved at Sullivan.

"Well, are you or not?" a voice called out from inside.

"Are I or not what?" Morrison answered.

"Coming in to see me!"

"I'm coming in to kill you!"

Sullivan left the barn, and ran to the right side of the house. He stopped, and looked around the corner at the porch so he could see it and the front door.

"I don't think so. I think you comin' in to die!"

Suddenly a woman screamed!

The front door flew open!

Mable Lee Priest ran out on the porch with a shotgun in her hand!

She turned, and pointed it at Morrison!

The bullet split her spine into as she dropped to the floor, the shotgun hitting the floor of the porch just as she did!

The shot was dead center of her back, right between her shoulder blades.

Sullivan never thought twice about killing a woman, never thought once. She should not have done it, should have known better.

He saw her crumpled body lying on the porch, and spit out toward the front of the porch.

Chapter 28

Sullivan looked over at Morrison, and saw him saying quietly the words – "What now?"

He then signaled for Morrison to pour the fire into the front of the house.

Morrison began shooting at the windows and door!

Sullivan turned around, held his rifle up to the side-window he was under as best he could, and opened fire!

He then signaled Morrison that he was going around to the back.

Sullivan ran toward the back of the house.

As he went past another window, he was showered with glass as a shotgun blast blew it out!

He kept running!

The same thing happened at the next window!

It was the last window. He stopped at the corner of the house.

He did not dare look around the corner. He knew there would be someone waiting on him, either Butch Coker or Ben Priest.

He heard more gunfire from the front of the house, both rifle and shotgun. He thought a minute, trying to decide what to do.

Sullivan propped his Winchester against the house, and then went back to the middle window. Most of the glass had been shot out.

He jumped up, getting both arms and shoulders up in the window. Then he managed to pull himself up into the opening. He crawled into the room as quietly as he could. He pulled his pistol from under his belt. He quietly moved across the room to the door leading to the hall. He threw his hat on the floor. He looked up and down the hall. No one was there where he could see him.

He knew one of them was waiting at the back door. He slipped down the hall toward the back of the house. When he got to the door, he saw Ben Priest standing there just outside on the back step. He pulled back the hammer of the pistol, and pointed it at Ben's head.

"Hey," he said.

Ben Priest turned to look up!

Sullivan fired his pistol at Ben's forehead!

Ben Priest crumpled to the ground!

Sullivan turned around quickly!

One more to go, he thought.

He slipped back up the hall toward the front of the house. He heard the continued shooting by Morrison and Butch Coker, neither one of them hitting the other.

When he reached the front room, he saw Butch Coker kneeling by the window to the right of the door.

"You can choose the easy way or the other easy way!"

Butch Coker turned to fire at Sullivan.

Sullivan fired two shots quickly!

Coker fell over in the floor!

"That was easy. Come on in Sheriff!"

Sheriff Morrison walked over to the steps, then stepped up on the porch, and then stepped over the body of Mable Lee Priest. He then stepped inside the house.

"That does it, I guess," Sullivan said.

"I'd say it is done. Good work."

"Ben is at the back door."

"Fine. That's all of them. I'll send the happy undertaker out here to pick'em up."

"What about the horses?"

"We'll have them sold. The money will pay for the burials."

"And the place here?"

"No next of kin, I don't guess," replied Morrison. "We'll let the bank take it and sell it. Put the money in an account or something in case some kin do show up. Ain't our concern no longer. Let's get out of here."

As the two lawmen rode back into town, they said very little. Both of them were quiet, absorbed in their thoughts. They did what had to be done. It was not their choice. Somebody else chose it. They had to kill them or be killed. It was always that way.

Still, five lives had been taken. Five human beings were now dead, and one of them a woman.

It was a terrible thing, but there was never time to consider that. The lawman who hesitates to consider the plight of the human race is the one who does not go home that night.

Point a gun at a lawman, and you will die. Plain and simple.

Chapter 29

Josephine saw Sullivan as he passed by the house headed to the barn. When he put his horse up, he then went in the back door.

"I'm glad you made it home all right. How did it go?"

"I killed a woman."

"What? Oh, Toombs."

"Shot her dead."

"What happened?"

"She was about to kill Morrison. That Priest woman. I had no choice."

"I'm sorry."

"Me too."

"Anybody else die?"

"All of'em. Dead."

"It must have been bad."

"It was for a while. That boy just wasn't comin' with us, and his whole family was goin' to make sure he didn't."

"Goodness."

"No. Badness. Real bad. A bad situation. Bad people. Bad day."

"I'm sorry."

"Tell me, how are you?"

"I feel really good."

"Don't over do it. Anything."

"Yes, Sir, Deputy."

"That's what I like to hear."

"Hungry?"

"Yeah. Killin' makes me hungry."

"I'll fix you something good to eat."

"Good. I got duty tonight."

Later that evening, Sullivan sat at the desk in the sheriff's office. He looked over a few wanted posters.

After an hour of that, he decided to walk down the quiet street to check out the lifeless town.

He heard the piano in Hart's saloon. When he looked inside, there were only a few people there. He went in, and stepped over to the bar. Pots Fuller saw him.

"Evenin', Deputy," he said, as he approached Sullivan.

"Hello, Pots."

"I heard about the shoot-out."

"That's what it was, a shoot-out."

"So, they were all willing to die to protect Butch."

"Well, no. I don't think it was that at all. They were all willin' for us to die to protect Butch."

"Even Mable Lee?"

"Yep. I was surprised by that."

"You the one that did it?"

"Yep."

"It must have been a tough decision?"

"Weren't no decision at all. Didn't have time to decide. I just reacted. When someone points a gun at ya or someone you are with, ya don't have time to decide. You just react. Those that think it through, got about two seconds left of their lives."

"So, even though she was a woman, you wouldn't hesitate to do it again?"

"Not at all. Seems quiet tonight."

"Yeah. It is. Real quiet. A man in my business can't make a living like this. I need some cowboys to come in here, and live it up, drink it up, shoot it up. Helps yore business too, you know."

"There are times when I like to be bored. That's why I left the Rangers. It was never boring. A man can take just so much excitement."

"Yes. I guess so. Still, I make my living off excitement."

"Right. I'm goin' on down the street. Check things out. If it gets excitin' in here, I will come back real quick."

"Sure. Be careful."

"Always."

As Sullivan walked on down the street, he kept thinking about what he knew. You cannot be careful. You do not have time to be careful. It is all instinct, reaction, reflex. To be careful is to die.

What a day – a day of instinct, reaction, reflex. It was the kind of day he had grown to hate. This is why he left the Rangers, this and his marriage to Josephine.

Now, here he was trying to find something different, and it was the same kind of thing all over again. The difference was he did not have to ride a hundred miles to find it, be confronted by it, be challenged be it, be threatened by it. He had to ride only five miles. The result was the same.

It was the same situation, the same danger, the same gun-fight, the same outcome. Lucky for him, the same outcome.

And then, there was the game being played out by the animal killer. Who could that be? Why?

Chapter 30

The sun had not been up long when Toombs Sullivan walked across the wide, dusty main street of Fort Worth, and headed up the hill to home.

He went in the front door, walked through the house, and found Josephine cooking breakfast.

"Coffee's made. Want some?"

"Badly. Need more than want."

"How was it?"

"A welcomed quiet night."

"Good. Be ready in a minute."

"No hurry."

When Josephine poured Sullivan a cup of coffee, he slowly sipped some of it.

"Are you feeling all right?" he asked.

"I feel amazingly well. I'm not sick at all today. So far."

"Well, good. Let's hope you're beyond all that."

"I hope so, but even if I'm not, I can handle that all right."

"I know. You're a strong woman."

"I'm trying to be."

"Have you looked out the back door?" he asked her.

"I have not had the nerve. Or the time."

"I have the nerve, and the time."

He walked over to the door, and slowly opened it. He stood there looking at the steps. Josephine wondered why he did not come right back inside.

"What is it?" she asked.

"Come and see."

She walked to the door, stood just behind Sullivan, and looked around his right shoulder.

"My god! A bear!" she exclaimed.

"You know your animals."

"But we don't know your enemy."

"We'll find out soon enough."

"Guess this spoils your appetite?"

"Let's eat," he rplied.

They backed up, closed the door, and sat down at the table.

"Is there no end to this?" she asked.

"Pass the eggs."

"Sure."

"Thanks."

"Need more coffee?"

"Please."

She poured coffee in his cup while he scraped some of the scrambled eggs onto his plate.

"No, we're not to the end of this. Better be glad too. At least we have some time to figure out what to do. If I can just do that. Figure out what to do."

Later that morning Sullivan tied a rope to the bear, got on his horse, and dragged the bear deep into the nearby woods back behind the house. He left him there for some animal to enjoy. Maybe it would be a mountain lion. Maybe just the buzzards. He did not care at all.

The bear was big, huge Sullivan thought. How could he have been put there in the night without somebody seeing something? Where was he killed? How can anybody kill a bear that size, and then get him into town? He was dragged by a rope obviously, just as he had dragged him away. But that was a lot of trouble, took a lot of effort. And why a bear? What did that mean? What did any of it mean?

When he went back to the office, he told Morrison what had happened.

"This is gettin' serious, Sullivan."

"It's pretty serious to me for sure."

"What can be done?"

"I'm goin' to sit up all night every night until I see who this is. I'll hide out in the barn. Don't come to our house after dark. Ya might get shot."

"I won't come a callin' after dark, I promise."

When Sullivan got home that evening, he told Josephine what he was going to do.

"You stay inside. Keep the doors locked. Do not open a door for anybody but me."

"Are you sure about this? It seems awfully dangerous."

"Of course, it is, but so is doin' nothin'. You know where the pistols are. You become concerned, get one of them."

"I will."

"You fire a shot, I'll come runnin'."

"Good."

"But don't shoot me."

"Never."

That night after the sun had gone down on over in the west, Sullivan made his way out to the barn. He carried with him his pistol and the Winchester rifle. The Sharps was more deadly, but it was one shot at a time, reload, another shot. In the dark, he would need several shots he thought.

Chapter 31

Sullivan slowly climbed up the ladder to the hay loft, careful to not drop the Winchester. He situated himself in the open doorway to the loft where he could look directly at the back of the house. He could look around both sides of the house somewhat so that he could see anyone coming from any direction except straight behind him. He hoped that would not be the case. Still, he would be able to see anyone approaching the house from behind the barn once they were under him.

He sat down, leaned back against a bale of hay, and made himself comfortable. He laid the Winchester down beside his right leg, and snuggled the pistol further under his belt.

He watched the lights go out in the house as Josephine cut them off.

He heard an owl hooting somewhere off behind him in the woods.

It was a dark night. The house was dark. The yard was dark. The barn was dark. He might not be able to see anyone very well, but he was sure no one could see him at all.

There was only one thing to do now. That was just wait. Wait for a sound, a noise, a shadow, a movement, a figure.

Stay awake. Don't get sleepy. Concentrate on the back of the house. Keep looking around, keep listening.

It was still early, too early. He knew that. But he had to be out there early so as not to be seen by whoever was coming.

Two hours went by. By then, his eyes were tired of looking. He realized he had been squinting. No need for that. Just relax. Quit trying to see something or somebody who is not there yet.

Suddenly he heard a noise. He listened closely. Where was it? What was it?

It was behind the barn. He was tearing through the limbs and leaves and undergrowth.

Sullivan reached down carefully. He picked up the Winchester. A bullet was already chambered. He pulled the hammer back slowly. He was ready to shoot and kill whoever it was.

The noise ceased. He was out of the woods now, and beside the barn, to Sullivan's right.

Sullivan waited. His breathing increased, his pulse rate increased, he had a jumpy feeling in his stomach, his mouth went too dry to spit.

Come on, come on, step out where I can see you. Go ahead to the house. Put something dead on our steps, and you'll be dead before you get it in place.

He saw a shadow move out from the side of the barn. Then there was a figure, a small figure, a short figure. It was too small to be a man.

It was somebody's old blood hound. A big dog, big enough to make all that noise, but he was not a man.

At least he had gotten Sullivan more awake, got the blood flowing, got the juices all stirred up.

Sullivan wondered what that dog was doing back there in the woods. Maybe he had found the bear. Maybe he was just making his rounds, checking out the woods for a coon or a possum. Guess he had found neither one.

More hours passed by. Was he coming or not? How long could he just sit there?

A ray of light fell across Sullivan's face. He opened his eyes, and saw the sun was up. He shook himself awake.

He had fallen asleep sometime in the early hours of the new day.

He looked at the back door. There was nothing there.

It was a good thing he had not come during the night. He would have gotten away with it again.

Still, Sullivan was aggravated with himself for going to sleep while on guard. In the army you would be in big trouble for that.

He climbed down out of the hay loft. When he went inside the house, he found Josephine in the kitchen already. She had the coffee on, and was getting breakfast ready.

"I looked out the door. Did not see anything. I didn't hear a shot in the night either, so I figured he didn't show up," Josephine said.

"No. He did not. And I didn't either. Good thing he didn't come around."

"What do you mean you did not show up?"

"Sometime in the early hours of the morning, I fell asleep. That was stupid."

"Don't blame yourself for that."

"I'm the one who did it."

"It's fine. We are all right."

"Just lucky."

Josephine smiled at Sullivan, and then said, "His luck is going to change."

Chapter 32

For the next seven nights Sullivan repeated the same ritual. Most of those nights, he managed to stay awake, only falling to sleep shortly before dawn. He got enough sleep to keep him going during the day.

Several weeks went by with Sullivan not spending the night in the barn. There was no further activity by the mystery person who brought the dead animals to the back steps.

It was late September now. The days were still hot, but not quite as bad as they had been. The air felt different at night. There was just the hint that a change was coming. The days were not as long. A few leaves on a few trees were beginning to change their color.

One morning, Sullivan sat in the office with Sheriff Morrison. They discussed the situation.

"Well, maybe it was just a harmless prank somebody was playing on you," Morrison said.

Morrison got up, and walked over to the stove. He poured himself a cup of coffee.

"Want some?"

"Nope. Had plenty at home this mornin'."

"I hope it's drinkable."

"Maybe it was a prank. But it's a little odd that he just stopped without any conclusion to this. He went to a lot of trouble. Then he quit. It just feels to me like it is not over, not finished."

"This coffee is terrible," Morrison said.

"Make some more."

"Yeah, but it's been weeks. If there was any conclusion to this, you would know it by now. Maybe it was some kid or a drifter or somebody who just gave up and moved on."

"I hope you're right. I hope I'm wrong."

"Too much trouble to make more coffee."

"I won't put money on it, but I think I'm right," Sullivan said.

"Maybe I will make some more."

"But what about shooting at me in the outhouse? That don't seem like a kid or a stranger. That makes all this serious, very serious."

"Yep, there is that aspect. I didn't think of that. At any rate, he hasn't come back."

"Not yet."

"I think I will make some more."

That evening, when Sullivan went home, he shared what he and Morrison had said.

"So, he doesn't think he will ever come back?" Josephine asked.

"Well, I don't know if he does or not. But he doesn't seem to think it is all that serious. Except the shooting at me. He has no answer about that, and I don't either. But that just makes this whole thing more serious. That's my thinkin'."

"I agree. A prankster would not be firing at you, even though it does seem he was not really trying to hit you."

"I don't know. I'm just not convinced it's all over. I just have a feelin', and it's not a good one."

"I hope you're wrong."

"Me too."

"Changing the subject, do you notice anything different about me."

"I do indeed. You are beginin' to show some."

"Yes, I am. Before long I will look like a real pregnant woman."

"Before you know it, that baby boy will be here."

"Or that baby girl. I'm not convinced it's a boy."

"What about names? Pick out any yet?"

"If it's a boy," she said with a smile, "he should be named Toombs, Junior. Don't you think?"

"Sure."

"If it's a girl Josie Agatha. That was my mother's name, Agatha."

"Well, that's a fine name. I like it."

"Good. So, are we settled on that? Toombs, Junior or Josie Agatha?"

"Yes. I like them both."

"All right."

"And how do you feel today?"

"I've felt really good. I have all kinds of energy. I cleaned the house. Some things I have neglected, I took care of today."

"Don't overdo it. You take care of yourself, and Little

Toombs."

"I will be very careful, and take care of Little Josie."

Chapter 33

The next morning, when Sullivan opened the back door to go to the outhouse, he found a large rattlesnake lying on the steps. It was obvious it had been placed there by someone.

So, now he's back, he said to himself. A snake. Why a snake?

Sullivan had been right all along. He was not done with this. Whoever this was still had a point to make.

When Sullivan came back inside, he lit a fire in the stove, and put the coffee pot on it.

He broke four eggs into a bowl. He then took a fork, and began stirring them around. He placed a frying pan on the stove, putting a little lard in it. When the lard melted, he poured the eggs into the pan. Soon the eggs were ready.

Josephine walked into the kitchen. She saw what he was doing.

"Oh, getting breakfast ready. Thanks. All help is appreciated."

"Thought I would give you a hand."

"Great."

"What kind of meat would like to have with these eggs?"

"What are my choices?"

"Bacon, beef steak, or rattlesnake."

"What?"

"Bacon, beef steak, or rattlesnake."

"That's what I thought you said."

"I did."

"Where did the snake come from? And no, I don't want any of it."

"The back steps."

"Back steps?"

"Yep. Found him when I first went out."

"You're not kidding me, are you?"

"Not in the least bit."

"He's back."

"It would appear."

"What do we do?"

"I have no idea. I guess I go back on night watch. See what happens."

"I hate this. I thought it was over."

"I never thought that."

When Sullivan reported to the office later that morning, he told Morrison what he had found on his back steps.

"That is odd indeed. Have some coffee. This is better than some of it has been. Have a seat, have a seat."

Sullivan walked over to the stove, picked up a cup, and poured some coffee in it.

He sat down in a chair across from Morrison's desk.

"Not bad," he said. "This is drinkable."

"Good. So, a rattlesnake, eh?"

"Yeah. Can't figger it out. Don't make sense, but none of this has."

"Let's see, ya got a snake, a bear, and what else?"

"A mountain lion and an eagle."

"None of them are domestic, no pets. All four are wild, and could cause injury or danger or something."

"Right. Is that a clue of some kind?" Sullivan asked.

"Could very well be. But to what? I mean, other than watch out, danger is near. It's a warning for sure."

"So, why the warning? If he's goin' to do somethin', why not just attack. Shoot me down on the street? Set the house on fire at night, and then shoot me when we run out? Why not that?"

"Because he is playing a game with you. He wants you to be afraid, to be suspicious, to always be on the lookout."

"He's succeeding. I am always on the lookout."

As they talked a boy suddenly came to the office. He stopped at the door.

"You Mister Sullivan?" the boy asked.

"I am."

"Mister Pots wants to see you. He said he got something you need to know about."

"Tell'im I'll be right there."

"All right. Bye."

"Well," Sullivan said to Morrison, "I hope this is something good."

"Reckon what it could be?"

"I have no idea. But Pots can be a source of a lot of information. I'll go find out."

Sullivan left the office, walked up the boardwalk to Hart's Saloon, and went inside.

When Pots looked up and saw Sullivan, he stopped what he was doing, and waved him over to the bar.

"Sullivan, I got something you need to know."

Chapter 34

Sullivan leaned over the bar a little, anxious to hear what Pots had to say.

"Well, Sir, this man came in here first thing this morning. He knew all about your snake that showed up."

"What? It just happened."

"Yeah. And he knew about the others, the lion, the eagle, the bear."

"How?"

"He has some kind of connection with that Comanche Joe Storm. This man is some kind of breed or full-blooded Indian or something. I don't know.

"Anyway, he said that Comanche Joe is after you for what you did. He is seeking revenge.

"He told me about those animals on your back door step.

They were not just randomly picked for no reason. The mountain lion is for a Comanche you killed named Fast Running Lion. The eagle is for Eagle That Flies Low. The bear is for Bear With Wings. And that snake is for One Who Crawls On Belly. He didn't tell me where or when any of this took place. He just said that in your fights with the Comanches you had killed all of these men. Many others, of course, but these four had some connection with Joe Storm. Maybe he grew up with them or maybe they were kin to him. He didn't spell that out, but was saying there was something special about these four."

"Of course, I have no idea when I killed any of them or where or who they were. I just knew at the time I had to kill them before they killed me. They were intent on that. I am here today because they are not."

"Oh, and another comment, Sullivan. He said something about the time has come. It will soon be all over."

"That sounds like he means business after all. It's not just a game of bringing me what he killed. I can only do what I have tried to do. Sit up in the barn loft all night, and wait for him to show himself."

"Oh, yeah, and he said tonight is the night. And something about a cow would be the sign."

"It's good to know that. I can be ready for him."

"Be sure you are, Sullivan. Be sure you are. I don't like this at all."

"I don't like it either. But thanks for all this. It's good to know something definite. See ya. I hope."

"Yeah, me too."

As Sullivan turned to leave, Pots added one more comment.

"Be real careful."

Sullivan went back to the office. Morrison was sitting at his desk.

"What did you find out?" he said, as he looked up at Sullivan.

"Comanche Joe Storm is the one giving us all the dead animals. Each one represented a Comanche I had killed. They were, uh, let's see . . . . Fast Running Lion, Eagle That Flies Low, Bear With Wings, and uh, One Who Crawls On Belly.

"And Pots said an Indian or maybe a breed came in and told him this, and that tonight Storm is coming after me seeking revenge."

"You'll be in the barn again?"

"Yeah. I figure that'll be my best shot."

"Why don't I come wait in the house? Two against him is twice as good as one. And I'll be with Josephine."

"Good idea. Thanks."

"So, what do we need to do today?"

"I think I should go on home. Get my guns cleaned up and ready, and get my ammo ready. Maybe you should be seen out in town just like everything is normal. Both of us maybe are being watched. We shouldn't tip him off that we are expecting him."

"But he knows you know now because of the message you were sent."

"Right, but he don't know you will be involved in this.

He knows I'll be getting' ready. But he don't know you will also."

"I'll wait until the sun goes down, and it's good and dark," Morrison said. "Then I'll slip up there remaining in the shadows as best I can. Be sure to tell Josephine not to shoot me. Leave the front door unlocked. I'll be there."

"Good. I'm going on now."

"Be careful. I'll see ya tonight after we kill him."

"Right," Sullivan said, as he left the office.

He walked up the hill trying to look around some, but not being too obvious about it.

When he reached the house, he went in the front door. He walked through the house, and found Josephine in the kitchen.

She was surprised to see him home that time of the day.

"What are you doing here?"

"I have something to tell you."

Chapter 35

Sullivan kept his eyes on the back of the house. He expected Comanche Joe Storm to try to come in that way.

He reasoned that people are like animals. They are creatures of habit. He had always come to the back of the house. He was familiar with it. He would come back that way. If not, Morrison was inside with Josephine, in case he did try to come in the front door. Either way, they were ready for him.

Sullivan, in the hay loft, had his pistol and his Winchester rifle. Morrison had his pistol and a shotgun, double barrel, twelve gauge. It could tear a man into. That was the intent. Josephine had two pistols. She was a good enough shot that she could defend herself quite well.

They waited. That was all they could do. There was no hurry up. Comanche Joe Storm would determine when the action began. It was totally up to him.

Sullivan sat in the dark in the hay loft of the barn. He had no idea what time it was. He thought it must be getting late.

Morrison looked at his pocket watch every twenty minutes or so. He knew it was getting late.

Josephine kept looking at the clock that sat on the cabinet in the kitchen. She and Sullivan and Morrison had decided that, at a certain point, she should turn out all the lamps and go to bed, not to sleep, but to make it appear to be a normal night. It was late. She did what they had planned.

Sullivan sat in the dark in the hay loft, and stared down at the back of the house, his Winchester ready.

Morrison sat in the dark by the front door, staring at it, his shotgun ready.

Josephine lay on the bed in the dark, staring at the ceiling, a pistol in each hand, both of them ready.

They all wondered how they could stay awake, waiting waiting, waiting.

The minutes slowly ticked by. The hours slowly dragged by.

Though the eyes became heavy, there was too much tension to fall asleep. But their minds had to be occupied with something, anything to make the hours go by.

Sullivan thought back over his time in the war. There were those long days and weeks of complete boredom when nothing was happening. Then they were suddenly interrupted by long marches, terrifying battles, horror and terror and fear and suffering and wounded men and men blown to pieces and screams of men having their legs and arms cut off. There was the terrible food and not enough of it and hunger and thirst. There was cold and heat and rain and snow and wind and warm fires and a nice blanket. There was victory and defeat and gain and loss and hope and despair. There was friendship and losing friends and compassion and mercy and love and hatred and vengeance and killing, a lot of killing. It was in the war that a farm boy learned how to kill, to kill and think nothing of it, to kill without feeling or regret or sorrow or hesitation, to kill even with a sense of joy and accomplishment. It all trained him well to become a Texas Ranger, for as a Ranger he could kill anyone, anytime, and think nothing of it, be it Comanche, Comanchero, bank robber, crook, killer, thief.

It had all prepared him, had gotten him ready, though he had no idea at the time it would lead him to be a lawman.

Then there was the real horror of coming home and finding his wife and son buried in the back yard. But then he had found Constance, not dead at all. What strange turns life can take.

Sheriff Morrison, sitting by the front door, had so many similar thoughts and memories about the war. He went to fight because Texas went to fight. His allegiance was to Texas. He would defend Texas against anyone and anything. That was his whole life, defending Texas as a lawman before the war, as a soldier during the war, and now as a lawman again. This Comanche Joe Storm was just another in a long stream of men, evil men, who thought they were a law unto themselves. They thought they could do anything to anyone anywhere anytime. He would have to be shown just like all the others. They would show him tonight. And the myth of Comanche Joe would be blown up. He had had his day. His day of judgement had finally come.

Josephine thought back about what brought her to Texas. She and her husband had bought the ranch. He came out to it first to set everything up, build them a house, buy the cattle, begin the herd. But after months she stopped hearing from him. When she came to find him, she discovered he had disappeared. She bravely carried on, and made the ranch a profitable operation. Kidnaped by outlaws, she was rescued by Sullivan and the Texas Rangers. Toombs Sullivan saved her life in more ways than one.

Who could fall sleep with such thoughts and memories dancing around inside a person's head? It was all enough to keep a person awake all night.

It kept Sullivan awake. He was still awake when the first timid rays of light slipped slowly across the eastern sky.

He climbed down out of the loft. He walked over to the house, went in the backdoor. Seeing no one, he went up the hall to the front room.

"My God!"

Chapter 36

Sheriff Morrison was lying on the floor, covered in blood. His throat had been cut. His abdomen sliced open. His scalp had been taken. Next to him was the bloody head of a cow.

Sullivan sank to his knees by Morrison, overcome by what he saw. He had seen plenty, but this was different.

Josephine! Josephine! Where is she?

Sullivan rushed into the bedroom, expecting to find her dead, but she was not there!

He looked at the wall on the other side of the bed. Written in blood on the wall was one word.

RANCH

He took her captive!

To the ranch!

Have to get there!

Hurry! Hurry! Hurry!

Constance is at the ranch!

He'll kill both of them!

Does he know about me and Constance?

What sick revenge!

Why not just kill me?

Why this?

Why them?

He knows it was Josephine's ranch!

He knows it now belongs to Constance!

How does he know all this?

What sick revenge!

What sick revenge!

Got to get there!

Hurry!

Sullivan ran out of the house, taking with him his Winchester rifle and also the Sharps. He made sure he had enough ammo for both of them.

He quickly saddled his horse, mounted up, and charged down the hill to the main street of Fort Worth.

He stopped at the office, and raced inside. He was almost out of his mind, but he managed to write a note for Pots.

"Pots, Morrison dead at our house. Josephine gone.

I have gone to get the killer, Comanche Joe Storm.

If I am not back today, please see he gets a

decent burial. I will pay when I return. Sullivan"

He took the road that went south. He would follow it the fifteen miles or so to the ranch. He rode hard and fast, as fast as his horse could go.

When he got to the ranch, he stopped a hundred yards away from the house. The place looked deserted. There were no horses in the corral. There were no cattle in the upper pasture. There was no sign of life. No one had been there for weeks.

He got down off of his horse. He took his Winchester in his right hand, and with his left led his horse to the water trough. He let him drink. Then he tied him to the fence.

Sullivan looked around again. No sign of life, just nothing, no one.

He saw signs where two horses had been ridden to the front of the house. Then they were ridden away.

He slowly walked toward the house. He stepped up on the porch. He stopped to listen. Then he opened the door. He knew the house well.

He walked through the front room toward the kitchen. He stopped, and looked in.

"Noooooooo!"

"God! No! No! No!"

Josephine was lying on the table!

Blood was everywhere!

She was naked!

She had been raped!

Her abdomen was sliced open!

Her throat was cut!

Her scalp has been taken!

Sullivan fell to the floor! He screamed! He wept! He screamed! He cried out! He rolled on the floor! He wept! He screamed! His body shook! He cried out!

He laid on the floor for over two hours, unable to move.

He no longer cried or screamed or wept or shook. He was not able to do anything any longer. He was cried out and screamed out and wept out and totally still.

He knew what he had to do. But he dreaded the thought of looking at her again. How could he? How could he touch her or move her? But he had to. He had to do it, and he knew it.

A blanket. He needed a blanket to wrap her in so she would not be cold. She was cold now with no clothes on. She needed to be warm.

He managed to stand up. He walked back through the house looking for a blanket, anything. He went in the bedrooms. There was nothing. There was nothing left in the house. There were no blankets. There was no furniture, no chairs, no beds, nothing, nothing except that long large table in the kitchen where Josephine was lying, lying dead and cold and alone.

He went out to the barn where he found several blankets in the room where some ranch hands slept.

He found a shovel. He went behind the barn where other people had been buried. They had all been murdered. He had buried them there. And Josephine would join them. They would be glad, glad to see her.

He dug the grave.

He went back inside. He wrapped the blankets around Josephine. He picked her up, carried her outside, and gently placed her in the grave. He slowly pulled the dirt over her.

When he finished, he stood there looking down at the dirt. He said a silent prayer, the kind they always had for fallen Rangers.

He went back in the barn, placed the shovel back where it had been, then walked back outside.

Then he saw what he had not seen earlier. There was a sign near the house. He slowly read the words on it.

Ranch for Sale – see Fort Worth Bank

Constance had left. But where did she go?

At least she was not there.

Chapter 37

Sullivan knew why he did it. He knew very well why Comanche Joe Storm had killed Morrison, took Josephine to the ranch, and then killed her there. He was drawing him out away from town, out to his own country, out where the Comanches lived, out to the wastelands where ambush was always easy and death was always hard.

Fine. Fine. Have it your way. Two can play this game. You must think you know this country better than I do. This is where I killed those four Comanches you are mad about, seeking revenge for them. I killed them here. They had no advantage over me because I knew their country as well as they did, and as well as you do.

Sullivan stood by his horse with these thoughts rushing through his mind along with a hundred others. He was almost in a trance, staring off at the horizon, looking at nothing, seeing nothing.

He blinked his eyes several times, looked down at the ground, and then spoke to his horse.

"This ain't goin' after him. Guess we best be gettin' on. You ready? Good. Me too."

He looked back at the house one last time. He got on his horse, rode down along the fence, turned left, and headed across the upper pasture. He soon reached the creek, crossed it, and then went across the lower pasture. He headed up the long hill.

When he reached the top of the hill, he stopped. It was obvious Joe Storm was leaving behind a trail that was easy to follow. So, he would follow.

It was mid-afternoon now. In a couple of hours, he would need to stop for the night. But what about food? In the rush, he did not anticipate such a trip as this. He brought nothing with him he could eat. And there was nothing at the ranch he could have brought with him. Then he remembered a rancher he had met. His place was not far off the trail he was following. George Major and his wife Christine had a small place just a couple of hours ahead. Maybe they would put him up for the night.

Late in the afternoon, he came to the place where he would turn west to go the ranch. But he noticed a troubling sign. Joe Storm's tracks turned to the west.

Sullivan hoped Storm was not headed to that ranch. He would know fairly soon.

When he got to the ranch, he stopped well back from the house. He pulled out his Winchester. He was a little nervous about what he might find. But things looked normal.

He dismounted, and walked his horse to the front of the house. He tied him to the rail. There was blood all over the porch. He knew what had happened. When he stepped up on the porch, the door suddenly opened.

"Toombs Sullivan. Am I glad to see you."

"George. Are y'all all right?"

"Yes. Oh, the blood. That's why I'm glad to see you."

"What happened?"

"We don't rightly know. I was inside earlier today. When I came out the door here, I found the head of one of our cows lying right there. Strangest thing. I figger some Indians wanted the beef, and put the head here to let me know they took it, and maybe they were trying to say they just took that one. I've had'em take cows before, ya know. But with them around here in this area, I'm a little nervous about it. Nothing calms the nerves like seeing a Texas Ranger."

"I guess so, but I'm afraid it ain't that simple."

"What ya mean?"

"It's a long story."

"Well, come on in. Chris about has supper ready. We'll feed ya. You can stay the night."

"Thanks. I was hoping you could put me up. I came off without any provisions. You'll see why when I tell ya what happened."

"Chris! Put out another plate! It's Ranger Sullivan! He's gonna stay the night!"

When they went back to the kitchen, Christine Major turned around to greet Sullivan.

"Why, Mister Sullivan, fancy seeing you out here. How are you?"

"I'm well. You?"

"Good."

"Call me Toombs. Mister Sullivan makes me feel older than I am."

"Sure. What brings you out here?"

As they sat around the table, Sullivan told his story of horror and murder. The Majors were shocked when they heard what he told them.

Chapter 38

George and Christine Majors were both in their fifties. George was tall and lanky. His face and hands were brown from the sun. There were lines down his thin face that reflected not just his age, but his long years of being out in the weather, working hard, trying to make a living on a hard scrabble ranch and farm. He had deep set brown eyes. His hair was partly gray.

Christine was a thin woman, with hair that had once been brown, but like George's, was now a mixture of colors and tints. She had a natural beauty that the years of toil and trouble had not destroyed, even though she had been aged by all of that.

"So, the cow's head is just leading you on?" George Majors asked.

"Yep, I think so."

"What did you do? Kill an Indian named Cow Head?" asked

Christine.

"Naw. It was something to get my attention, get me to the ranch."

"And why did you quit being a Ranger?" she asked.

"It's a hard life, being a Ranger. Ya have to go out for days and weeks at a time, sleep on the ground, ride all day, chase Indians and outlaws, get shot at by people who want to kill ya.”

“Kind of like you’re doing right now,” she said.

“Exactly. I thought I was through with this, but here I am. But the main reason was I wanted to marry Josephine. That was what did it.”

“I’m really sorry,” Christine said, as she placed her hand on top of Sullivan’s.

“Yeah. Me too. She was a fine woman. I guess the shock of it hasn’t set in yet. The reality will hit me when this is over.”

“I wish we could help you,” George said.

“You are helping me. A fine meal, a place to sleep tonight. That’s the help I needed. I thank you for it.”

Sleep did not come to Toombs Sullivan that night. He could not keep from thinking about what had happened. He had seen too much. It was too vivid, too real, too up close, too personal.

The next morning, he could smell the coffee boiling and the bacon frying. He got up, got dressed, and went in the kitchen.

“Morning,” Christine said. “Sleep well?”

“Oh, yeah. Slept well.”

“Good. How you want your eggs?”

"In my stomach. How they get there, and what they look like doesn't matter to me."

"I'll scramble them up then. George is checking on a cow that's about to have a baby. He'll be back in a minute."

Sullivan sat down at the table. In a few minutes, George came in just as the meal was ready. When they were finished eating, Sullivan thanked them for their hospitality.

"And I need to get goin'. Don't know what the day will be like or how long this will take, but I need to get after him."

"Sure, we understand. Be careful out there," George replied.

"And remember, you always have a place here with us," Christine added. "And here, take this. Some food for your journey. It's a few biscuits, some ham, a piece of cake."

"Thanks. I will remember. And thanks for the food."

George walked with Sullivan out to the barn. When his horse was saddled, Sullivan shook George's hand.

"Thanks again."

"You bet."

With that, Sullivan headed out following the tracks that were still clearly visible.

Two horses, one rider it appeared. The tracks of one of them did not look like there was anyone on it. They were not as deep as those of the other horse.

What's he doin' with two horses, Sullivan thought, unless he is riding hard and fast, and not wanting him to catch up with him?

But he thought that was the point, letting him get close enough to him for Joe Storm to kill him.

He must be going a long way. He must have some special place for this to happen.

All he could do was follow him. Follow, follow, and wait and see what happens. Not a very good way to die.

Chapter 39

Sullivan had not seen any place where Joe Storm had stopped for the night.

After riding for two hours, he came to a creek. There it was, the place where he camped.

Sullivan got down off his horse, and tied him to a small tree. He walked over to where Storm had made a fire. He put his hand down on the ashes. They were still warm. He could not be too far ahead of him.

He let his horse drink water at the creek. Then he mounted up, crossed the creek, and kept following the tracks of the two horses.

He will be somewhere waiting on him. It must be a game he was playing. He was leading Sullivan on toward some kind of trap. It was not just about killing him at all. It was getting the most pleasure he could out of this, inflicting the most pain and torture.

Maybe he was out there waiting behind a tree or a rock or just over a hill. Maybe he will shoot at him from some distance. Maybe he will never see him, just feel a bullet going in. Maybe he will not feel it at all, just fall over dead. That is always the best way. No pain. Just nothing. Just be dead, and never know what hit you. Quick and easy, real easy.

A little more than an hour later, Sullivan came to a place where he saw a cow's head hanging by a small rope from the limb of a large tree. There was a lot of blood on the ground under the head.

He stopped, got off his horse. Then he walked over to the cow's head. He looked around on the ground.

An arrow whizzed by his head!

It stuck in the tree!

He ducked down!

He pulled his pistol from under his belt!

Another arrow struck his horse!

Just under his front shoulder!

The horse fell dead!

He saw no one!

Screaming!

An Indian charged at him with a tomahawk!

He swung it at Sullivan's head!

Sullivan ducked, charged the Indian, ramming his shoulder into his waste!

They both fell to the ground!

They rolled on the ground, each one trying to subdue the other!

Sullivan pulled his knife out of his boot as he jumped up!

The Indian had a knife!

He slashed at Sullivan!

Sullivan threw himself at the Indian, rolling on the ground, knocking him over!

With both hands he raised his knife in the air and lunged at the Indian, driving the knife deep into his chest!

He heard the knife going in, crunching bones. With some effort, he pulled it back out slowly. Blood gushed out. The Indian's eyes were wide open. His mouth was open with a grimacing expression. Blood came out of it.

He was a Comanche for sure. Some friend of Joe Storm.

Why did he do this? Why have this Indian waiting on him? Why not just do the killing himself? Maybe it's a test, an aggravation, a warning? Maybe he expected him to kill him? Follow on to the next trap, the next test?

Sullivan walked through the brush, undergrowth, and small trees. He looked around until he found the Indian's pony.

He began wondering if he had been followed. If there was this one, then surely there must be others.

Sullivan untied the pony. He led him over to where his horse was lying on the ground.

With great effort, he managed to get his saddle off his horse. He put it and his own bridle on the pony.

An unshod Indian pony. Not a bad idea. He was sorry about his horse being killed. But now on this Indian pony he would be safer. Any Indian coming up behind him would not know he was following a white man. It was a blessing in disguise, the killing of his horse by that Comanche. But somebody might see his dead horse. He would just have to take a chance, and hope the next one would not have been back that far.

The next one. The next one. Surely there will be others.

What could he do? Nothing. All he could do was just follow his tracks, see what happens next, react quick enough to stay alive.

That's it. Stay alive. Stay alive, and get some good old-fashioned revenge. Sweet revenge, the kind that comes from a perfect hatred.

Chapter 40

Sullivan was more careful now. He not only looked ahead, he tried to look all around. He tried to look on the other side of large boulders while they were still ahead of him, strained to see over hills before he reached them, attempted to look behind large trees to the left and the right, both at the same time.

Often, he stopped to listen. He listened for any unusual sounds. He listened to birds to be sure they were still singing, and not scared away. He listened to the wind.

He smelled the air to see if there was a campfire near him, to see if there were any unusual odors, to catch the scent of horses, ponies, cows.

So far nothing was out of place, out of order, unusual, unexpected.

It was late in the day. The shadows were lengthening. The sun was slipping low beyond the distant western hills.

Sullivan had to find a good place to camp, some place out of the wind, for the nights were cooler. He needed a place with a little protection.

He found a place nestled up against a hill. There were thick trees on two sides. It would be cozy enough, and hopefully safe enough.

He tied the pony to one of the trees, and took off the saddle. There was nothing there for the pony to eat, nor was there any water for the pony or himself, but he still had some in his canteen. He would find grass and water for the pony the next day, he was sure. At least that is what he told the pony.

He placed his saddle against the steep lower side of the hill. There was no need to build a fire. He had nothing to cook anyway. It would be safer with no fire for anyone to see. He sat down, leaned back against the saddle, and opened the bag of food. He ate two biscuits, a piece of ham, and the cake, saving a biscuit and a piece of ham for breakfast the next morning.

Sleep. Sleep. He wondered if he would be able to sleep. He wondered if he should sleep. There just might be somebody out there wanting to slip up on him. His horse would probably have alerted him if that were the case. He didn't know about the Indian pony. He did not trust it even though he had promised him grass and water the next day.

He had eaten the food slowly, hardly tasting it at all. He knew it must have been good. His mind was too full to think about food, and how it tasted.

He knew that, just like the night before, he would probably not be able to sleep. There was too much to think about. The pain of what had happened was still there, even more intense perhaps. Josephine and the baby and Morrison gone, just gone. No sense to it at all. Why them? Were they just in the way or were they just bait and was he just taunting him to draw him out away from town, away from any help of any kind? Maybe he wanted to get him back to the place where he had killed those Comanches. But where was that? He never knew their names or if they even had names. He did not care. It could be any place between Fort Worth and Austin or San Antonio or over to the west or down near the badlands.

He would find out if some Indian did not kill him during the night.

He stared out into the darkness where he saw nothing. There was no wind. There were no moving shadows. There was no noise of any kind.

He wondered what the baby would have been, a boy or a girl? It was never given a chance to live. Only a crazy man would do such a thing as that.

He thought about what it would have been like to live a long time with Josephine. They could have had a good marriage of many years. They could have grown old together. She was such a fine woman. He loved her dearly and deeply.

Just taken away from him in the blinking of an eye.

Then there was Morrison. He was such a good sheriff, such a fine man. He enjoyed working with him, getting to know him.

And then Constance. What about her? What had happened to her? She just disappeared. She just sold the place right away and left. Who knows where she went? Back to Georgia he wondered?

He yawned a few times. He must not go to sleep. It was just too dangerous. Too much could happen, come slipping up on him.

He heard the early morning birds as they announced the coming of a brand-new day.

He opened his eyes enough to see the first little rays of light as they made their way through the limbs of the trees.

Chapter 41

Sullivan stood up, stretched, looked at the pony.

"Yeah, I know. I made you a promise. Today, today. I don't have any water left either. We'll find it or we'll both die. We'll die together all right?"

He ate the last biscuit, the last piece of ham, and then drank the last three swallows of water.

Then he put the saddle on the pony. He led him out away from the hill and the trees.

"Time to move on, young man, or is it young brave, young Indian pony? You don't have any idea what I am sayin', do ya? No speak'a de Engless."

Sullivan stood still for a few moments, looking, listening. He saw nothing out of order, heard nothing unusual.

He mounted up on the pony. Then he turned him south following the tracks.

Almost an hour later, he came to a creek. He stopped, looked around, then got off the pony.

He led the pony to the water to let him drink.

He took off his boots and hat. He took his pistol from under his belt and laid it on his hat.

He waded out into the creek where he sat down with only his head out of the water. He ducked his head under, then came back up. He thoroughly soaked his clothes and himself. It was good to feel clean again.

Clean again. How could he ever be clean again with all the blood he had spread all over a good bit of Texas? But yes, he thought, it was always me or them. And he was going to spread some around again before this was all over.

He looked over at the pony. The pony had lifted up his head, and was looking at Sullivan.

"What? You never seen a man in the water before? Get used to it, Indian brave."

When Sullivan came back out of the water, he led the pony over to a place where there was some grass. He let the pony eat while he laid down on the grass in the warmth of the early morning sun.

He stayed for over an hour, letting his clothes dry some.

The pony was still munching on the grass.

"Time to go young Indian brave, pony."

He got back on the pony, crossed the creek, kept following the tracks.

Two hours later he came to a campsite. He knew this was where Comanche Joe Storm had spent the night. He could tell from the tracks there had been two horses there.

"Indian pony, he is still a few hours ahead of us. Tonight, if we don't stop, we could just keep going, and ride right up on him. That would catch him by surprise. But, of course, the surprise just might be on us. He might be expecting us to do that. Let's don't. Good. But at some point, he will stop, and wait on us. Stop and wait."

On he rode further south, always south, always following the tracks.

Shortly after noon, Sullivan came to a place thick with willow trees and young white oaks. He stopped to look and listen. There was something about that place he did not like.

Suddenly he heard a flutter of wings. A covey of quail flew up just in front of the trees. He was not close enough for him to have caused that. There was somebody in there.

He turned the pony to his left. He went over behind a small rise, dismounted, and tied the pony to a tree.

He pulled out his Winchester.

Bending low, he circled way around to his left. It was his favorite tactic, one he had learned during the war. He had done it so many times as a Ranger.

He moved slowly, close to the ground, one small step at a time. He entered the thicket. There was no sound from anyone. But he knew there was someone in there. It was instinct that told him that. And his knowledge of how Indians think. He knew what they did.

Inching forward, he could not see anything. He could not hear anything.

Slow, slow, slow. Move slowly if it takes all day.

He was not in a hurry, and had nothing better to do. Why rush it?

Then he saw him. A Comanche for sure and for certain. He was crouching down behind a tree.

Sullivan raised his rifle, pointing it right at the Indian's head.

But then!

Chapter 42

The full weight of somebody slammed into Sullivan!

He knocked him over!

They rolled on the ground together!

There was a knife in his hand!

Sullivan held to both of his hands!

Still the knife came close to Sullivan's throat several times!

He managed to push him away!

He jumped to his feet just as the Indian did the same thing!

The Indian rushed toward him!

Sullivan pulled out his pistol, and shot him in the face!

The Indian fell to the ground!

He heard something tearing through the thicket behind him!

He turned around!

It was that first Indian he had seen!

He was running, running fast!

He had a tomahawk in his uplifted right hand!

Closer! Closer!

Thirty feet away!

Sullivan pointed the pistol at him, and pulled the trigger!

The bullet went through his neck!

He fell in a clump to the ground!

Sullivan whirled around, looked all around, making sure there was no one else.

That was it. Two of them this time. He wondered if there would be three next time?

He left the thicket, and went back to the pony.

He mounted up, went around the thicket, picking up the tracks again.

Two hours passed. He came to a small creek. He let the pony drink. He dismounted, bent down low on one knee, and drank the water. It was cool. He filled his canteen. He walked around a little, letting his blood circulate, and letting the pony rest.

Then he mounted up, crossed the creek, followed the tracks.

The tracks still led south. Down south was good Indian country, good Comanche country.

Sullivan began recognizing certain landmarks. He knew this country. He had been there before.

It was a hard place. It was difficult on man and beast. He was out now away from grass for the pony, and water for both of them. It was a land of barren hills and lifeless valleys. There were good places to hide for an ambush, good places to kill, good places to die. But it worked both ways. He could kill his enemy as easily as his enemy could kill him. And that was his intent. Would it be Comanche Joe Storm next time? Or would it be three Comanches? He would find out, maybe sooner than later.

Soon he had to go through a narrow pass between high walled hills. He did not want to do it, but he had no choice. He sat there on the pony for a few minutes, looking ahead. It was impossible for the pony to go up over the hills on either side. If he tried to go around, it would be way around. He would lose time, the day, the tracks.

He knew the place well. He was not about to go riding through the pass, not yet. He would have to look around very carefully first.

He had climbed up the left side before where he had a good shot. He could see well up there. He would know very quickly if this was an ambush.

He got off the pony, hoping he would not wander off. He took with him the Sharps. He might have to make a long shot. Better that than up close. Up close was too close.

He began climbing very slowly. There was no rush. To rush sometimes meant to die quickly. He had plenty of time.

He inched his way up the hill. When he reached the top, he lay flat down. He crawled up to a boulder that was about two feet high, maybe six feet wide and long. What a great place from which to shoot.

He looked straight ahead. He saw no one.

This flat-top hill was about two hundred yards long, both sides. So, the pass through it was that long as well.

He thought surely this would be the place. But he kept looking. There was just no one there. And there was no one on the other side either.

Then down at the far end on his side, he saw a man stand up. It was a Comanche, he was sure. The Indian waved at someone on the other side.

Sullivan looked over there. The Indian on that side suddenly stood up. He waved back.

The words raced through his head – take the shot, take the shot, take the shot.

He propped himself on the bolder. He aimed carefully. He took a deep breath.

Chapter 43

The Comanche sat down quickly, as did the one on the other side.

Sullivan knew he had waited too long, aimed too long, breathed too long. There was only one thing to do. He would have to crawl toward him, hoping he would stand up again.

He looked ahead. There were other boulders out in front of him. He needed to get to the next one which was a little to his left, thirty to forty feet ahead.

He crawled forward, made it without being seen. He looked ahead to both sides. They were still down. Only one thing to do, keep crawling.

The next boulder was much larger, maybe four to five feet high. He could get up and run to it if he stayed close to the ground. They would never see him.

When he got behind it, he stayed down for a moment. Then he slowly stood up, looking over it.

He stood there almost twenty minutes. He knew they would stand again. It enabled them to get a better view of the pass as they checked to see if he was coming through it.

The one on his side stood up. Sullivan braced his arm on the boulder, pulled back the hammer, aimed, held his breath.

He pulled the trigger!

The Comanche never even heard the shot!

He was dead before the sound waves reached him!

He collapsed where he stood!

Sullivan looked quickly to his right across the pass to the other side.

Little chips of rock jumped up in the air to his left! The bullet hit the boulder and went flying past him!

He saw the other Comanche over there duck down.

He reloaded the Sharps quickly, pulling down the lever, cocking back the hammer, and putting a bullet in it.

"Rise up again. Try that again. I'll put a stop to ya."

He waited, looked, waited. He wondered if he was changing position, seeking a better shot from a better angle.

Then he saw the top of his head moving along behind rocks and boulders.

Trying to get around behind me, eh, Sullivan thought.

We'll see about that.

He moved around to the left side of the boulder. The Sharps was cocked. He braced himself. He pointed the Sharps at about where he expected the Comanche to be.

He saw him look up over a large rock.

Sullivan aimed, pulled the trigger!

A clump of hair and scalp and blood flew back away from his target!

"Two down now. Is there another one or not. If you are here come on out and show yoreself."

He heard a horse galloping through the pass. He ran over to the edge, looked down, and saw the third Comanche riding as fast as he could, leading his pony away.

He reloaded quickly!

He aimed the Sharps at the middle of his back!

He pulled the trigger!

The Comanche fell off his pony in a heap!

Both ponies kept running, disappearing out the other end of the pass!

"Come back here, you wild Indian pony!"

Sullivan spit on the ground, as he held the Sharps in his left hand by his thigh.

"Or go on home, back where ya came from. How about leaving my saddle out there where I can find it."

Sullivan knew he had to catch that pony. He only had two more shells for the Sharps in his pocket. Six in his pistol. That was it.

He went up to where the first Indian was lying on the ground. He picked up his Winchester. It had a sling on it. He put the rifle over his shoulder. He took the Indian's ammo belt, and put it over his other shoulder. He knew that would help.

He walked to the far end of the ridge, climbed down, and looked back up the pass. He walked up the pass to where the Comanche was on the ground. He also took his ammo belt.

Then he turned around, headed out of the pass.

He might find that pony real soon. It might take the rest of the day. He might not find him until tomorrow or the next day. But he would track him until he found him. He still wanted his saddle. He did not want to be out in that country on foot. He would find him no matter how long it took.

Unless the Indians found him first.

Chapter 44

Sullivan walked out of the pass, looking straight ahead at what awaited him. It was miles and miles of nothing, nothing but barren land. He knew there was better land further on with water in several creeks, but he would have to survive long enough to get there.

He looked down at the tracks before him. There were the tracks of Comanche Joe Storm. These were the ones he wanted to follow. They were easy to follow. But there were other tracks he needed to follow instead. He had to first of all find that Indian pony, the one with his saddle. At that moment, that was the most important thing for him to do.

He saw two sets of unshod Indian pony tracks. They veered off to his right, toward the west. Joe Storm's tracks went straight south.

There was only one thing to do. He went after the ponies.

It looked like they were still running. He wondered how long they would run. He hoped not long.

After nearly three hours he stopped to rest. He sat down in the shade of a tree, for he was in a different terrain now. Maybe there would be water not too far ahead.

Perhaps he would be able to kill some game, a deer, a jack rabbit, a bird of some kind, or maybe find fish in a creek or a river.

Then he remembered his matches were in his saddle-bags. He had never been able to rub two sticks together to start a fire. He was no Indian. He was a white man, and a white man needed his matches.

The thought of having to eat something raw was repulsive to him, but he might have to do it anyway. For some reason raw fish was a little more appealing to him. He thought he could handle that.

After a good rest he began walking on further.

Almost an hour later, he topped a small hill. He saw the Indian pony standing near a small river eating grass. The other pony was nowhere to be seen.

Sullivan walked slowly toward the pony so he would not spook him.

The pony looked up and saw him. Then he put his head back down, and continued to eat the grass.

Sullivan walked up to him, took the reins in his left hand, and with his right, he patted the pony on his neck and shoulder. He led the pony over to a tree where he tied the reins to a limb. The pony was still able to eat the grass.

He then sat down, took off his boots and belt and hat, waded into the small river, and sat down. He drank water, submerged his head. Then he got out of the water. He walked over to the green grass, laid down, and looked up at the blue sky. He closed his eyes. Sometime later he woke up.

Food, he had to have food, anything. He thought about trying to catch a fish with his hands, but that could be difficult.

He hooked the Indian's Winchester over his saddle horn. He secured his Sharps rifle. With his Winchester, he walked down the river a little way.

He had not gone far when he saw a large jack rabbit. He was near the river. That was supper.

He wanted to be sure to shoot him in the head so he would not destroy him. He knelt down, took careful aim, squeezed the trigger.

Ten minutes later he had a fire going. He sat near the river as he cleaned the rabbit. Soon it was cooking over the fire.

Sullivan was concerned about the sound of the shot and the smoke from his fire. In a way, he was inviting trouble.

But he had to eat. If trouble came, he would face it.

When the rabbit was almost ready to eat, Sulivan heard a voice call out.

"Hello the camp!"

"Come on in."

Sullivan did not think an Indian could sound that much like a white man. But just in case, he placed his hand on his pistol.

In a few moments, a man leading his horse walked into the camp.

"Howdy. My name is Henry January."

"Welcome. I'm Toombs Sullivan."

"You the Texas Ranger I heard about?"

"I used to be."

"Used to be Toombs Sullivan, or used be a Texas Ranger?"

"I'm still Toombs Sullivan, but no longer a Texas Ranger."

"If you ain't no longer, what you doing out here?"

"I'm a Deputy Sheriff from Fort Worth now. I'm chasing a bad man."

"I'm a bounty hunter from everywhere. I'm chasing a bad man. Who you after?"

"Comanche Joe Storm."

"Well, I am a donkey's uncle. That's who I am looking for."

"Sit down. Have some rabbit."

Chapter 45

Sullivan told Henry January what had happened, starting from the beginning with the dead animals. He then told him about Josephine and Sheriff Morrison. That was why he was out there trying to find Comanche Joe Storm.

"I see," Henry January finally replied. "It's real personal. I can see that. It ain't personal with me. It's economics. There's a two thousand dollar bounty on his head. I'm a bounty hunter. It's what I do. I just care about the money. That's all."

Sullivan looked at Henry January as he sat on the other side of the fire. He was a big man with sharp facial features, dark hair, a full dark mustache that curled around his mouth. His skin was dark, but maybe just from being out in the sun so much. His pants were tucked into boots that were high, almost up to his knees. He wore a dark shirt, buttoned up to his neck, and a dark brown coat. His hat was wide-brimmed and black.

"Maybe we could work together," Sullivan suggested.

"You mean put together your personal reasons with my economic concerns?"

"Yep. That's what I was thinking."

Henry January spit in the fire, and said, "I think we got us a partnership."

"Good."

"Say, what you doing with that Indian pony?"

"Joe Storm has had some of his Comanche friends attacking me all along the way. First one. Then two. Then three. They killed my horse. I took one of theirs, this pony. I've killed all of them so far."

"I gathered as much. Least-wise you would not have gotten this far."

"Changing the subject, tell me about yourself."

"Born and raised right here in Texas. Grew up on a little ranch. One day, this was before the war, these raiders came to steal our cattle, horses. They killed my folks. I was off down in the far pasture. I saw smoke, thought I heard gun-fire. By the time I got to the house, they were gone. I buried my folks. Then I went after them. It took me two weeks to find them. But when I did, I killed them. I had heard there was a bounty on them, three of them, two hundred dollars a piece. So, I took them in, and got the money. It was the first money I ever made. And it was easy. I decided I could make a living at that, not have to sweat it out working with a bunch of stinking cows.

"Then the war came along. I went like everybody else. I was at Gettysburg. That's where we should have won and ended the war. But we didn't. They won, but did not end the war because they let us escape back into Virginia.

"As soon as I got back to Texas, I took up bounty hunting again. I always favor the ones that are wanted dead or alive. I just as soon kill'em as look at'em. Now this Joe Storm, he is what I call high-class bounty. Real bad, wanted real bad, and the money is real good.

"Here I am. What got you to this point in life?"

"I grew up on a little farm in north-west Georgia. Me and my wife had a boy and our own place. I went to fight too. When I came home there were two graves in the yard. I left there, and came to Texas. I became a Texas Ranger because I had nothin' else to do. I sort of fell into it by saving the life of a Ranger Captain in a saloon. I was down south a while, but then got transferred up to Dallas. Rangered for several years.

"To make a long story short, I wanted to marry a woman, Josephine. I was tired of Rangerin' anyway. Became a Deputy in Fort Worth.

"This Comanche Joe Storm, like I said earlier, fancies himself gettin' even with me for killin' some of his Comanche friends.

"The strangest thing is I met my first wife at her ranch which had belonged to Josephine when I first met her.

"Her name is Constance. She didn't die at all, but she thought I did. The graves I found were our son and a

Yankee soldier. Thinking I was dead, she married a man. They came out here. Bought that ranch. He was killed. She sold it I guess, and left. Don't know where she went."

Henry January thought for a moment, looked at Sullivan, then spoke.

"Well. That is pretty bad, tragic. You lost two wives, even though one ain't dead, she's still lost. Me, I decided I didn't want any attachments. It's easier that way. I don't answer to nobody, and nobody answers to me. I go when I want to, and where I want to. That's my for better or worse. Sometime it is better. Sometime it is worse. But when it's worse, it's just me that takes it on the chin. I don't have to worry about nobody else."

"I see the wisdom of that," Sullivan replied.

"Well, Sir, all that aside, what's going to be our plan?"

Chapter 46

The next morning Sullivan and January headed out south-east. Sullivan had explained how he had been following Joe Storm's tracks directly south. But they decided rather than go back to pick up the tracks, they would cut across, and see if they could find them further on down, or maybe run into Storm, catching him unawares.

They had gotten an early start, neither one of them slept very well if at all. January had with him enough food for them to eat breakfast. However, that would soon run out. They could eat in the middle of the day if they wanted to, but that evening they would be living off the land.

Sullivan had an idea where the tracks would be. Sometime after nine o'clock they came to them.

"This is it," he said. "See, two horses. Look closer, you'll see one of them has no rider."

They dismounted to look at them close-up.

"You are so right, my Friend," said January.

They rode hard from there, hoping to gain ground, maybe catch up with Joe Storm.

Forty-five minutes later they came to a river. It was the Brazos River.

Sullivan and January dismounted to let the horses drink. They filled their canteens.

"The Brazos," Sullivan said.

"Yeah. You know what the word means?"

"Can't say that I do."

"Early Spanish explorers gave it its name. The Spanish phrase is Rio de los Brazos de Dios. It means the river of the arms of God."

"Well, how did you learn that?"

"I grew up about a mile from here to the east. We came here a lot."

"Then you're at home."

"Yeah, just about."

"Have any bad feelings about being here, with what happened and all that?"

"No. I guess not. I got my revenge. That took care of the anger and hatred. They were dead, so I didn't have them to hate anymore. And I made some good money out of their deaths. I let go of anything that was bad. I have such good memories about growing up here. We had such a good life. It was hard, but it was also so sweet and good. If you don't let go of bad things, evil things, they will eat you alive from the inside out. So, you decide to let go and live, rather than hang on and grieve to death."

"Yeah, I know you're right about that. That's why I came to Texas, to get the past out of my system."

"That's good. And you'll have to do that again now because of all this."

"Yep. I know."

"Ready to cross?"

"Sure."

They mounted their horses, and crossed the river. They stopped when they reached the other side.

"You see any tracks?" January asked.

"Not a one."

"He went either up or down river."

"I'm guessin' down, but why stay in the river if he would assume we would keep headin' south anyway?" Sullivan asked.

"He may well have gone up the river. Playing some kind of game. What this is all about anyway ain't it?"

"Yes, it is. And I'll tell ya somethin' else. He now knows I am not alone. He did this to split us up. He has known we are together I bet since last night."

"That means he saw me come into yore camp," January said.

"That means he has been closer all along than I thought. Either him or some of his Comanche friends."

"Well, I'll go up river a while and take a look. You go down river. The one who sees tracks fires two shots. Any more than two, and the other will know something more than tracks was found. Something like trouble."

January headed up river along the river's western banks. He rode slowly, looking closely for any sign that Joe Storm had come out of the river somewhere up that way.

However, he thought it was unlikely that he had done that. He probably went on south down-river.

Sullivan had watched January ride off. Then he turned his horse south-east to follow the river, riding along its bank. He thought it was most likely that Joe Storm had gone in that direction.

Almost twenty minutes later, Henry January stopped abruptly.

He heard two shots!

Then three more!

"Oh, no!"

He turned his horse around quickly!

Chapter 47

Henry January rode as fast as he could back in the other direction down the river. He knew Sullivan was in trouble.

When he reached Sullivan, he found him standing over two dead Comanches.

"What happened?" January exclaimed.

"They jumped me! There's two more on foot! Com'on!"

Sullivan ran off through the small trees and undergrowth along the river.

January charged through them on his horse.

The Indians were running fast. They reached their ponies, jumped on them, and rode away before Sullivan and January could catch up to them.

"I'm going on!" January shouted, as Sullivan went back to his pony.

Sullivan found his pony drinking water at the river. He mounted him, pulled the reins back away from the water, and rode hard to catch up.

He could hear shots being fired, but neither January nor the Indians were being hit for they continued to ride south.

In a few minutes, Sullivan saw January riding back toward him.

"Turn around!" January shouted.

"What?" Sullivan yelled back, as he held up his pony.

"They're coming!"

"Who?"

"You'll find out if you don't come on!"

As January charged past Sullivan, he pulled his pony around, following him quickly.

They headed back toward the river. When they reached it, they went right across to the other side. They dismounted quickly, ducking down behind a fallen tree.

Over fifteen Comanches came riding out from where the trees were on the other side of the river.

Sullivan and January began firing their Winchesters!

Comanches began falling off their ponies!

Some fell on the bank of the river!

Others fell in the water!

Still others dismounted, disappearing in the tress and undergrowth!

"They'll cross the river up or down it and flank us!" Sullivan shouted at January.

"Any bright ideas?"

"Yeah! You go up! I'll go down. We'll meet'em!"

"Wonderful."

"Stay low."

While January moved up the river, Sullivan went down it, staying low, close to the ground. He hid behind a large bush. He waited. He put more shells in his rifle.

Here they came!

Three of them!

When they were fifteen feet away, he jumped up, quickly shooting all three of them!

They fell to the ground in a single clump!

Sullivan waited to see if there were others. There were no more.

As he turned back toward the direction in which January went, he heard someone shooting several times. He hoped it was January. He replaced the bullets he had just fired with three more. There was only one way to find out what had happened.

He moved through the undergrowth, not knowing who he would encounter. He stopped to listen.

Then he heard someone coming toward him, pushing aside the limbs of the bushes.

He raised his rifle, ready to shoot whoever it was if it was the wrong person.

Then he saw January, just as he spoke.

"You all right, Sullivan?"

"I am, and I see you are."

"I am. We know one thing now," January said.

"What would that be?"

"They all know we're coming. There will be no surprise whenever we arrive at our destination, wherever that is."

"I'm afraid you're right about that. This was a welcome party. Just one band of Comanches. Likely there are others out there waiting to greet us."

"I'd just as soon not be welcomed. They can just keep their hospitality to themselves."

"I agree," Sullivan replied. "I think this shows us the connection and influence Joe Storm has with these people. Might be good for him. But it ain't good for us. We're in his country now."

Chapter 48

"Sullivan, we need to think this through," said January, as they mounted up.

"Sure. How you see it?"

"We can't take on the whole Comanche nation. There's too many of them out there. I've no doubt we could kill every one of them that comes at us, but we gonna run out of ammo right soon. And we are already out of food. We better be trying to kill something to eat instead of just trying to kill Indians. I've as yet seen one I'd be willing to eat."

"You're so right. What say we follow the river on down? We'll find a place to camp for the night, see if we can shoot some supper, and maybe see where Storm crossed the river, if indeed he did."

"Fine by me," replied January.

"Let's stay on the east side of the river. At least we can keep it between us and any Comanches that might be on the other side."

"Good. Lead out."

The two men moved out away from the growth around the river in order to make the going easier. They rode slowly and deliberately. They kept their eyes and ears open, always alert. They listened out for the singing of the birds. As long as they could hear the birds singing, they figured they were all right. They watched for any flock of birds suddenly flying up and away, any quail being spooked.

They kept their eyes also on the ground, always looking for Joe Storm's tracks. They had to come to them soon.

Late in the afternoon, they came to what they thought were his tracks. They dismounted, looked closer.

"See here," Sullivan said. "This horse right here had nobody on him. It's Joe Storm for sure."

"I think you're right," January responded.

"He crossed the river right here. Headed on down. I just wish we knew how far he's goin' to lead us."

"I expect we'll be finding out."

"How about we camp here for the night? We got water here for us and the animals. All we need now is meat."

"Think we'll be all right building a fire?"

"They know where we are. If they want us, they'll come get us. But I don't think they'll come tonight. In the morning on across will be a good place and time for them."

"Yeah."

"You build us a fire," Sullivan suggested. "I'm going back off to the east; see if I can find us some supper."

"I'll be anxiously waiting."

Sullivan rode away in search of something they could eat. He worried about firing a shot. It would be an announcement of their location, but so would the smoke from their fire. He decided to not worry about either one.

Soon he came to a long and wide grassy area. It was along a small creek that flowed into the Brazos River he assumed. It looked like a good place for deer.

He got off the pony. He tied his reins to a tree back out of the way at a place where he hoped deer would not see him, if indeed there were any deer around. He intended to find out.

He slipped back to the grassy plain. He walked slowly along the edge of that area down toward the creek. He began seeing deer tracks. He was right in thinking they came there to eat the grass, and also to drink water from the creek. It looked like a good spot. He would wait there.

He could be wrong, of course. Maybe they would not show up at all. He could sit there until dark, see nothing, kill nothing, and eat nothing.

The day began fading away as the sun hurried on home out there in the west. The little shadows began growing now to their full maturity. They were bigger and bigger, and they began stretching out long and far.

Sullivan listened intently, looked closely.

Then fifty-plus yards away he saw two does hop out of the undergrowth.

His pulse began to quicken. Maybe he could hit one of them.

Surely a big buck would be behind them, maybe more does as well.

He wondered what he should do. Should he shoot one of the does or wait on the buck?

The buck would be much bigger. But he would be more than they could eat. Besides he would be producing more offspring if he left him alone. The smaller doe looked to be about the right size for him and January. No need to waste meat they could not eat before it ruined.

The does moved along slowly, nibbling at the grass, looking up, nibbling at the grass, looking up again.

The smaller doe was walking along behind the larger one.

Sullivan held up his Winchester, leveled it off, took aim, squeezed the trigger.

January suddenly looked up.

Chapter 49

When the meat was done, Sullivan reached over with his knife, and sliced off a piece of it. He took a bite out of it.

"It's good. Help yoreself."

"Don't mind if I do," replied January.

They both ate the meat silently for a while. Then Sullivan broke the silence.

"Ya know, I been thinking," Sullivan said.

"Is that good or bad?"

"I don't know. You tell me. I'm thinking they gonna be expecting us to keep following the tracks. That's where they'll be waiting."

"Expect so," January agreed.

"Why don't we sweep around toward the east some? We could come back into the tracks further down. We could cross the river in the mornin', then make a slight turn. We might find Joe Storm further on down, and leave his Comanche friends sittin' around waitin' on us."

"Good idea. That was good thinking after all."

They rotated watch during the night. Sullivan took the first watch while January tried to sleep, but with little success.

The night was clear and cool. Sullivan watched the stars. They were high up, and far beyond his imagination.

The moon was big and round and yellow-looking and close to the earth. There were no night sounds, only the almost silent flowing of the river. The horse and the Indian pony were calm.

Now and then Sullivan put a couple of pieces of wood on the fire, just enough to keep it going for it was not needed for its warmth, just for a little light.

There were very few shadows for there were no tall trees by the river, only the small ones that grew there.

So, neither Sullivan nor the animals were spooked by them.

After a while, Sullivan began to wonder if it was too silent. Maybe there should be shadows. Maybe there should be noises of some kind.

He put two more pieces of wood on the fire. Then he picked up his Winchester, and walked through the undergrowth and small trees to the edge of the river.

He stood there waiting and watching and looking at the light of the moon on the water.

He thought it would be just like Comanche Joe Storm to come slipping up on them during the night, just the way he had back in Fort Worth. He was an evil man and a sly man. He was tricky and smart.

Sullivan could see up and down the river very well. If Joe Storm crossed the river, he could kill him easily. If he saw him.

Sometime after midnight Sullivan went back to the fire.

January heard him.

"I'll take it," January said. "Maybe you can have better luck than I did trying to sleep."

"I doubt it. I been watching the river, just in case."

"Case of what?"

"In case we have visitors or a visitor."

"You expecting company?"

"Nope. That's when ya need to look for it, when you ain't expectin' it."

"I see what you mean."

As the sun came slowly creeping along the eastern horizon, the two men were awake for they had been waiting on the sun for some time.

They laid slices of the venison on the warm rocks around the fire. They let the meat heat up some. Then they ate it.

They packed up some of the meat that was left so they could have it the rest of the day and in the evening.

They saddled up the horse and the pony. They kept their Winchesters in their left hands, thinking they just might need them suddenly. They mounted their rides. Then they crossed the river.

When they reached the other side, they turned to the east to face the now fast rising of the sun. It was bright in their faces, making it difficult to see.

Less than a mile later, they turned back south.

They took their time. They were afraid they might go riding into something or someone they were not prepared to face.

They knew Comanche Joe Storm was out there somewhere setting a trap of some kind for them. They would find it or be in it soon enough. Why rush?

Chapter 50

Sullivan and January continued riding south for about five miles. They were cautious and slow and deliberate and very aware of their surroundings.

Years of fighting Comanches had taught Sullivan to be in touch with his own senses and with the land he traveled over. He had learned to listen, keep his eyes open, look ahead of where he was while keeping an eye on where he had been. He had learned to listen to his intuition, his feelings, his hunches, his suspicions.

At that point, they turned back west hoping they would either come upon Joe Storm's tracks or perhaps intercept him on his way south. They rode for about a mile.

There was something that was not right, Sullivan suddenly felt. He did not know what it was. It was as if there was something in the air. He could not identify what it was. He just knew he had a bad feeling.

They slowed their pace, moving cautiously along.

Sullivan looked all around, but could not see anything that was unusual or out of place or not natural.

He held up his hand for them to stop. He nodded at January and dismounted. January did the same.

He handed the reins of his pony to January, signaling for him to remain there while he walked ahead. He took his Winchester with him.

Sullivan bent low along the ground as he made his way toward a small hill. When he got to the top, he crawled to where he could look over beyond the hill. He saw two horses on the plain. They must be the ones Joe Storm was riding and leading. But he did not see Storm anywhere.

He decided to wait there a few minutes to see if he would show up. He lay there at the top of the hill, well concealed between rocks and boulders and small bushes.

He wondered where Storm could be and what could he be doing?

He kept waiting, kept looking, kept listening. But there was nothing, just the two horses standing alone.

He was startled by a noise behind him!

It was the Indian pony!

He was running right at him!

Sullivan jumped up!

He held up both arms!

The pony slowed!

Sullivan grabbed the reins!

Something happened, but Sullivan had no idea why the pony had gotten away, and run off away from January.

He led the pony, running back to where he had left January.

He first saw January's horse.

Then he saw January!

He was lying on his back!

A Comanche spear was stuck in his chest!

He was dead!

Sullivan whirled around, ready to fire his rifle.

There was no one there. He pulled the spear out of January. He knelt down, and placed his hand on January's neck. There was no pulse.

Sullivan wanted to bury January, and not just leave him there, but he had no shovel. He decided he would just pick him up on his way back, if he came back. He did not have time to bury him anyway. It would take too long. He had to go after Joe Storm at that moment, and not waste any time at all. They had caught up with him, and now was the time to kill him.

Sullivan reached down and took January's pistol from his holster. He might need it. January did not need it any longer. He stuffed the pistol in his belt on the opposite side from his own.

He jumped up on the pony, turned him around, and raced back to the hill. He rode right up to the top of it, looked down onto the plain where Joe Storm's two horses had been.

They were gone, and he was gone.

Sullivan charged down the other side of the little hill.

He had finally caught up with Storm. He would catch him now, and put an end to him.

His double set of tracks were easy to follow. He could not be that far ahead.

Sullivan kicked the pony in his sides and urged him on faster and faster. Surely, he could catch a man riding one horse and trying to hold onto another.

Chapter 51

Even as he pursued Joe Storm, Sullivan knew he was continuing to be led along. It was a trap. The whole thing was a trap. Anyone Sullivan was with had been killed in order to keep him in the pursuit, keep him coming after Storm. But there was no one else now. He was completely alone. The trap was set down there somewhere. He would ride right into it.

Was there anything he could do? He had tried what always worked for him, going around, coming up behind or at least to the side of whoever he was facing.

It did not work this time. It cost January his life.

So, what now? Sullivan thought. What would it be this time? How would he avoid whatever it was?

Then Sullivan realized he was thinking too much. He was asking himself too many questions he could not answer because there was no answer.

What he had to do was concentrate on the task at hand. Follow the tracks. Try to catch up with Joe Storm. Stop thinking, just be ready, just react, just trust his gut. Ride hard and fast and catch him.

He kept pushing the Indian pony forward, and the pony kept responding. The pony had been born for this. He could run all day.

The wind blew in Sullivan's face. The dust and sand and grit was in his eyes and in his mouth.

Sullivan had no time now to listen or look or try to read the signs. He only had time to ride faster and faster and faster.

Then he saw it!

It was one of the horses!

Joe Storm had let go of it!

Sullivan knew it now!

He knew Storm knew he was being caught up with!

He was running!

He was scared!

He was running scared!

A scared man will make mistakes!

Just stay after him!

There were hills ahead!

Steep hills!

When Sullivan reached the first hill, he stopped and dismounted. He looked at the ground. Joe Storm was off his horse, on foot now, leading his horse up the hill.

Sullivan did the same. His Winchester was in his right hand now as he led his pony with his left.

It was a steep climb up the trail as both he and his pony slipped and slid in the sand and pebbles and small rocks.

This had slowed Joe Storm down. Sullivan knew it, but it had slowed him down as well.

He kept trying to look up the trail, up the hill. Maybe Storm was up there taking aim at him. It was a trap. He knew it. He was walking, climbing, sometime almost crawling right into it. But he had no choice.

There was no way around this, no way to circle around and come up behind or beside him.

Sullivan knew he was wrong. Joe Storm was not scared and not running scared at all. He was leading Sullivan into his trap. But what was it? Where was it? How long was this going to take?

Sullivan caught himself asking questions again, questions he had no time for and no answer to.

On he and his pony climbed toward the top and toward possible death and toward his end and toward defeat.

After long hard difficult tiring straining minutes that seemed like they had stretched into hours and days, Sullivan reached the top.

He looked out down a narrow valley that ran between the steep rocky hills.

There he was!

He was riding fast!

But not that far away!

Maybe a shot!

A miracle shot!

A once in a lifetime lucky shot!

Sullivan put down the Winchester and took his Sharps from the saddle.

He knelt down behind a large boulder.

Joe Storm was three hundred yards away at least.

He pulled back the hammer!

He aimed!

He tried to lead him!

He pulled the trigger!

The horse went down!

Chapter 52

Sullivan watched as Joe Storm rolled on the ground as his horse tumbled over. He got up and ran for the hills beyond.

Sullivan quickly mounted the Indian pony, and charged down the hill chasing after Storm.

By the time Sullivan reached the dead horse, Storm had disappeared into the hills. But he saw where Storm went. It would not be hard to follow him.

Sullivan feared Storm would shoot his pony, his ride back to civilization. He jumped off him, letting him wander off on his own. He would find the pony later, if he could, if he survived this encounter with Storm. He intended to do just that.

He ran up the hill that Storm had climbed. It was steep and rocky, but a horse could make it up it, and Sullivan could see that many had in the past.

Sullivan kept looking up the trail, wondering when Storm was going to begin shooting at him. He was ready for it whenever it came.

The dirt kicked up just beside him!

It was to his right!

He heard three more shots!

The bullets whizzed past him!

They were close!

Just over his head!

He thought he could feel the heat of them!

But not really!

He thought he could smell them!

The burning gunpowder!

But he did not!

He lay flat on the ground, trying to look up the trail to see where the shots came from.

Then he saw Joe Storm running on ahead!

Sullivan jumped up and ran forward!

Two more shots!

The bullets hitting the ground beside him!

Then Sullivan realized Comanche Joe Storm was just not that bad a shot. He was missing him on purpose. He was trying to get Sullivan to follow him, just luring him on like he had all along.

That meant he had something up there that he wanted to get Sullivan into. It would be a way of getting his revenge, making Sullivan pay for what he did, pay in the worst way.

Sullivan stopped being concerned about being shot. He stood up and ran as fast as he could, up the hill, up the hill, up the hill!

He wanted to get to the top as quick as he could, and get this over with, whatever it was.

Then he saw it near the top of the hill. It was the opening to a cave. Joe Storm was in there.

Sullivan ran up to the opening, moving quickly to the left side of it. He stood there a moment, wondering what to do next.

He heard the voice of Joe Storm from within the cave.

"Come on in, Mister Sullivan! Don't be bashful now!"

"Why should I? I'm doin' fine right out here! You're the who is trapped now!"

"Oh, come on! Don't be like that! Be a good Ranger! I won't shoot, I promise!"

"Somehow I don't believe you!"

"I have laid down my guns! Just look inside! You'll see! We need to talk!"

Sullivan eased toward the opening of the cave. He slowly looked around it so he could see inside.

There stood Comanche Joe Storm with his hands held up shoulder high. He did not have a pistol on him that Sullivan could see. His rifle was off to the right side of the cave leaning against the wall.

Sullivan did not want to talk. He only wanted to do one thing. That was kill Joe Storm immediately.

He knew he should not do it, but he stepped in the cave anyway. He took four steps inside.

He saw Joe Storm for the first time. He was not like what anyone had ever said about him. He had sharp Indian facial features, dark skin, black eyes, his long hair was shoulder length. He wore no hat now, but his clothing was that of a white man. His black pants were tucked in his high boots, his shirt was blue, his coat was dark gray.

Sullivan stared at him for a moment.

Joe Storm jumped to his left!

He kicked something!

Sullivan was up the air!

Upside down!

He was caught in a rope net!

His rifle fell through the rope!

He could see Joe Storm rushing toward him!

A large knife was in his hand!

Sullivan pulled his pistol from his belt!

Joe Storm drew back the knife!

Sullivan shot him in his stomach!

Joe Storm fell to the ground, writhing in pain!

Sulivan pulled his knife from his right boot, and cut his way out of the net. He fell to the ground. He stood up, and stepped over to Joe Storm.

Joe Storm managed to speak.

"You see that rack over there . . . . it's what I had planned for you . . . . Texas Ranger. By now . . . . you're supposed to be on it. I was going to cut you up worse than I did that wife of yours. Mister Texas Ranger."

Sullivan looked over to his left against the wall. There stood the rack, maybe eight feet tall, four to five feet wide.

Sullivan knelt down beside Joe Storm.

"You know Joe Storm, there's a price on yore head, a big price. You know what it is, don't ya? Well, I don't want the money because I have you. I am going to do to you what you did to my wife and the sheriff. I'm goin' to cut yore throat, but first I'm goin' to slice open yore shirt, pull yore pants down just a little, and rip you wide open from yore gut to yore throat. Then I'm goin' to scalp you. Then I'm goin' to drag you out of here, and leave you outside so the buzzards and the coyotes and the rats can eat ya. How does that sound to ya? You like that?"

"Go ahead and do it, white man. If you got the guts."

"Oh, I got the guts, but you won't for long. I'm gonna do unto you what you have done unto others. Say good bye."

Sullivan cut open Joe Storm's shirt, pulled his pants down a little, and stuck his knife in his abdomen. Then he ripped it up his torso. He put the knife to his throat, and sliced it open. He pulled the front of his hair up, and scalped him.

Sullivan took hold of Joe Storm's right foot. He dragged him out of the cave. He threw the scalp on the ground. Then he looked down at Joe Storm. He spit on him.

Sullivan went back inside to get his Winchester.

He walked down the hill.

Chapter 53

Sullivan found the Indian pony waiting on him at the bottom of the hill. He was nibbling on grass. He walked up to the pony, took the reins, and patted him on his neck.

Then he dropped the reins, walked over to the edge of the hill, and collapsed. He began weeping uncontrollably. He had had no real chance to mourn the death of Josephine. His grief and sorrow and the horror and the pain and the terror and the loss had all built up inside of him. He lay flat on the ground on his stomach. He cried out. His hands clutched at the sandy dirt and the green grass.

Then he felt a nudge in his ribs on his left side. He turned and saw the pony standing over him. He stood up. He patted the pony again. He pulled himself together.

"Thanks for waiting on me, young fella," he said as he mounted him.

Sullivan headed out for Fort Worth. As he rode along, he realized he had felt perfectly at home. It was so natural, what he had done the last few days. He had blocked out what had happened in Fort Worth and at the ranch. He thought he must have just been in a trance of some kind. He had automatically done what he had done for years while fighting Indians. He hardly had to think what to do. He just did it.

It was odd to him. He had settled down, had gotten away from being out for days and weeks in hostile territory hunting hostile Indians and being hunted by them. He had turned away from all of that in order to become a family man again. He became a deputy in a town. That was what he wanted to do. He thought he had adapted very well.

Then he was pulled back into Indian fighting, being gone for days, sleeping on the ground, eating whatever he could find and kill.

He almost hated to admit it to himself, but this is what he was good at. He was good at Indian fighting.

It meant something. It counted for something. The mission of the Texas Rangers was to protect settlers from the Indians. That was important. If they did not do that, then who else would?

Yes, there was the Army and the forts they were building. But they could only do so much. The Rangers were still needed.

Now that Sheriff Morrison was dead, there would need to be a new Sheriff. And just who would that be? It would naturally fall to him. There would have to be an election, of course. But nobody would run against him. He would be elected.

Elected to do what? He would spend his time rounding up drunks and an occasional bank robber. Anybody could do that. Not many men could be a Texas

Ranger. He was a Texas Ranger. There was no use trying to run from that.

Then there was the house. He could never live there again. There were too many memories, and some of them were bad. He could not do it.

Days later Sullivan arrived back at the ranch. He had found Joe Storm's other horse, and had placed January's body on it. He had taken him to the ranch where he buried him beside the others. He placed his own saddle on that horse. Then he set the Indian pony free. He patted him on his neck one last time.

"You can go on back home now. Thanks for helping me, but you don't belong in my world. Go on now."

Back in Fort Worth, there were several things Sullivan had to do.

First was a funeral service for Josephine. It was held the day after he was back. The Methodist circuit riding preacher held the service at the cemetery.

Then he asked the bank to sell the house, and put the money in the account he and Josephine had shared.

Leaving the bank, he walked across the wide street to the telegraph office.

"I need to send a telegram to Dallas."

"Sure. Sorry about your wife, Deputy. It was some mean business. Glad you got him."

"Yeah, me too."

"Who does this go to?"

"Captain Jack Rice. I want to join the Texas Rangers again Stop But not up here Stop Josephine was killed Stop I got her killer Stop Please have me sent back south again Stop Yours Stop Toombs Sullivan Stop

The End

www.ingramcontent.com/pod-product-compliance
Lightning Source LLC
Chambersburg PA
CBHW071504140726
47997CB00005B/1851